What Goes Around Comes Around

A Small Town Girl With Big Time Problems

Effie L. Jones-Robinson

Illustration By: Jerry Jones

authorHOUSE®

AuthorHouse™
1663 Liberty Drive
Bloomington, IN 47403
www.authorhouse.com
Phone: 1-800-839-8640

First published by AuthorHouse 6/22/2009

ISBN: 978-1-4389-7449-1 (sc)
ISBN: 978-1-4389-7450-7 (hc)

Illustration By: Jerry Jones

Printed in the United States of America
Bloomington, Indiana

This book is printed on acid-free paper.

Acknowledgments

I would like to thank God who is the head of my life and for keeping me safe and forgiving all my sins and me not being as faithful to him as he has been to me.

I give a most special thanks to my sons Ronell M. Barnett and Brian Cunningham Jr. for making me a proud mother. No matter what was going on I could always feel their love and support. I love you both with everything in me.

To my Granddaughter, Ron'Neisha Barnett who the Lord took to glory early. RIP, I Love You.

A special thanks to my beautiful granddaughter for bringing me joy, Ron'Naijah Bankhead, granny love you baby.

Thanks to my mother and father who have been with the Lord for many years, Benjamin E. Jones and Zella W. Jones, I love and miss you both deeply.

Thanks to my sisters and brothers that is with the Lord also, making the best journey of their ever existing. Frankie L. Reed. Crystal M. Emory, Ben E. Jones and Willis Jones, I love you all very much.

Thanks to my other sisters and brothers that have given me much love. Zella S. Weatherspoon, Charles L. Jones(Josephine) Terry L. Jones, Jerry B. Jones(Patricia), Major Jones, Amos E.

Jones, Gwendolyn J. Jones, Jacqueline Jones, Sidney Jones, Devonda E. McTyer, I love all of you unconditionally.

A special thanks to my acting parents that I could always go to when I had a problem or just wanted someone to talk to or needed a good laugh, Bishop Carlton L. Johnson and First Lady Mrs. Irene Johnson, AKA Mommy and Poppy. I love you

And thanks to my family at Faith Congregational Church of God and Christ in Muskegon, Michigan for keeping it real and boosting me alone while writing this book and having the faith that it will be a great success.

Thank you Shane Buckley for always giving me the pep talk I needed when I almost gave up. I love you.

Thanks to you Brian Cunningham Sr. for always loving me, I love you

Thanks to my real friend of thirty years that was always there for me. Being a true friend means the world to me and encouraging me alone the way. You are a friend to the end. It's rare to have a real friend, we all know that. I love you Girl. Carolyn R. Diggs.

Honorary thanks to my friend that was always smiling at his first crush. You made a girl feel good. I know you are still singing to the LORD. I miss you. RIP Charles Williams Jr. AKA Ricky. I love you.

Posthumously thanks to my love, Ricky Dean Moore that I miss so much. You brought so much love in my life. I thank you for riding out my depression and anxiety and panic attacks while you were here. It's still hard letting you go. You are my inspiration for this book I love you and miss you to the max. RIP my love.

Chapter 1

It all started in the small town of Amity, Arkansas forty three years ago. To the union of Mr. and Mrs. Benjamin Jones, Effie Lagretto Jones was born. I had the blessing of being the fourteenth of fifteen children. There were eight boys and seven girls. Yes you read it right, eight boys and seven girls. And no, there were no twins, triplets, nor any adoptions. We were all single births.

Mama and daddy also raised one of their granddaughter's. Her name was Teresa she was raised just like us. No one would have known the difference if they weren't told.

The small town of Amity was a dark, dusty, dirty place we called home. There were no street lights; or should I say road lights. The only lights you would see were the ones from automobiles that would occasionally come alone. In the day time you could see as far as ¾ of a mile in each direction. That has since been rebuilt with houses, condominiums and paved streets.

Our home was a small two bedroom shack. That was home for us. I love and miss that small wood frame little house on the prairie type home, I wish I could go back in time when I didn't have a care in the world and the only thing I worried about was what mama was going to be cooking for dinner.

Our home was surrounded by cotton fields on all four sides. It was fun playing in the yard with my sisters and brothers. There were never all fifteen kids living in the house at one time. I had older sisters and brothers. They were grown and had moved out with their husbands and wives.

With our home only having two bedrooms, all of the girls slept in one bedroom and the boys slept in the other. Our mother and father slept in a bed in the living room. Our only source of heat was also in the living room, besides the kitchen stove.

In the winter I liked to see the red hot fire and hear the crackling of the burning wood. The heat coming from the fire was like a cozy fireplace. The warmth of the family sitting around the heater is a memory I have never forgotten. Sometimes it seemed like I could hear my brothers chopping wood on a big three stump in the back yard.

I miss going down to the levy trying to catch crawdads. I loved to climb trees, go fishing, and jump rope. I never learned how to jump double-dutch. I remember playing in the dirt and making mud pies.

We lived on an old plantation. My mother worked as a maid in the big house. It was 1/2 a mile away and daddy was a farmer for the people who owned the land. Now that I am older and wiser I can see that it was a plantation. The owners of the land were white. They lived in a big brick house. The black people picked cotton and were paid cheap wages for the hard work that they performed.

The cotton pickers always came to our house to get a cold cup of water from our pump, it had to be primed to even get water. The pump was our only source of water. I can vision the pump pouring out clear cold water without iodine (a necessary supplement that would come to haunt me later in my life.)

I used to wait on some of the cotton pickers to give them water. I use to love it when they came over to our house. I always felt so bad when I saw those people hot, sweaty and tired.

I was glad I was too young to work in the fields. My older sisters and brothers had to pick and chop cotton. A few of my brothers had to drive tractors like my daddy. Mama use to wash our clothes on the front porch in a washer called a ringer washer. Mama used to scrub our clothes with a board called a scrub board, until her hands would cramp. We had to carry water in a bucket to wash clothes, take baths and cook.

I remember thinking we were rich when we got water put into the house. We took baths in an aluminum tub called a foot tub. We had to take baths in our bedroom without much privacy.

Our bathroom was also outside. We never did get a bathroom in the house. It was six feet high and four feet wide. It was called an outhouse. There was no way of flushing the toilet so our bathroom had to be moved a few times a year. I use to be so afraid to use the toilet because I thought a snake would come up from it. At night we had to use a bucket, which was inside the house, we called it a slop jar. Once again, not much privacy.

Chapter 2

In front of our home was a steep curve, people use to try to bend the corner on two wheels. A few tried to, but they flipped upside down, including my oldest brother. His car flipped upside down and he crawled out the car and walked in the house, he didn't even have a scratch on him. When he came in the house he ate an onion so when the police came they couldn't smell the whiskey on his breath. Back then, there were no breathalyzer test, technology has came a long way. There's not much you can get away with today.

Our house was not very steady when it came to storms. When a tornado came through we had to run to the closest neighbor's house for shelter. Their house was about one mile away. If we couldn't make it to their house we would lie down in the closest ditch for shelter.

I always liked storms, they seem so cozy. They seem to bring calmness you know what they say "music calms the savage beast". I think a good storm does also. Sometimes I pray for rain. The night time is my favorite time of the day to relax. Mostly everyone was at home and you didn't have to worry too much about anyone coming by or calling.

I used to love to see a colorful rainbow; I wonder was there any gold at the end of it. In the winter we didn't have much snow but the ice storms were bad. I use to love to see snow in Arkansas, because we didn't get a lot. But, now I don't want to ever see it again, well maybe on Christmas day, but not after that.

The little town of Amity only had a little corner store. We also had a candy store that was back in the woods. We use to buy candy, cookies and moon pies. Do you remember those long boys? They also had potato chips and sodas; the soda was outside in a coca-cola cooler. They ran a Juke Joint that sold beer and whiskey.

I remember watching television in the living room. We only had three channels; we couldn't wait until Saturday came because we got to watch soul train, hee-haw and wrestling. My mama use to enjoy watching wrestling with her friends.

Daddy always made me laugh because; when he watched wrestling and boxing he would box in the air like he was actually fighting. Daddy would make ugly faces, he was always quiet. Watching him while he was watching wrestling was about the only time I saw daddy get excited.

We had a garden with mustard, turnip and collard greens. We had corn, and the biggest red juicy tomatoes, okra, peas and cabbages that grew almost as big as a basketball. Mama even grew the sweetest strawberries I had ever tasted.

We also had two pigs, one named Sara and the other one name was, Toe-Joe. I remember one beautiful Saturday morning mama told us not to go outside for a while, I being hard headed; I was going to go out anyway. I soon found out why she didn't want us to go outside. When I opened the back door I saw daddy with a butcher knife in his hand, he was getting ready to butcher Sara. He had Sara hanging from a tree. Daddy sliced Sara down the middle of her stomach, I cried all day. But that cry didn't last long, because when Sara turned into bacon, sausages, pig feet, pig ears, and ham, I quickly forgot all about Sara.

We also had lots of chickens. I loved to see baby chickens running around in the back yard. They were so cute and yellow. When the baby chickens were small they were called bitties, and then as they got bigger they become white.

Mama use to cook us flap jacks, in case you are wondering what flap jacks are, they were homemade pancakes, bacon, eggs and homemade syrup. No matter what was going on mama and daddy made sure we ate well.

Mama always cooked the best meals in town. On holidays she would cook homemade cakes and pies. Her jelly cakes were made of her home made jelly. I remember we use to sit around the table to see who would get to lick the bowl, spoon and the mixer. Mama's cakes were so tall and moist they would make your mouth water. It almost seems as if I can smell Mama's cooking now.

Friends came from miles around when they knew my mama was going to cook for the holidays. Some say that I cook just like her, but I think my other sisters' cooking is closer to Mama's cooking than mine, who am I to argue?

Like chitterlings, I don't know why anyone would eat something that smelled so bad. I tried to eat some a long time ago. I got a small piece and drowned it in hot sauce and put it in my mouth. As fast as I put it in my mouth I spit it out even faster. I never tried to eat them again. I used to cook some for my husband on Thanksgiving and Christmas. It would take me all day to clean twenty pounds of them. You know as a person tests their food for proper seasoning, I wasn't about to do that. I don't have anyone to cook them for now. I kind of miss that part of my life. It was a blessing to have someone I could cook for.

I used to love it when my family would get together. We all would cook a lot of different foods. We would barbecue ribs, chicken, steak, hotdogs and polish sausages. Mostly, the men would do the barbecuing. The women would cook the greens, corn on the cob, potato salad, cornbread, candied yams and an assortment of cakes and pies.

If you were underweight, when you came, you sure wouldn't be when you left. I miss those times. We were kind of poor but we were rich in love. On Christmas our presents would be an apple, orange and an assortment of nuts and candies.

Chapter 3

Mama and Daddy had these friends, they were the Watson family. They were a strange family. My family was close to the Watson's. They had a lot of kids. Back then families were large.

Mr. Watson was very different. He used to walk around the house with no clothes on. His wife Mrs. Watson was just as different. Most of the family was a bunch of super freaks with the exception of maybe two. One of my brothers had a son by one of the girls. She and one other were the only ones with a little since. One of my sisters's liked one of the boys until he got mad at her and put his fist through my parents' wall.

One day all of us kids went to the Watson's house to play while mama and daddy went to the store. I was about eleven years old. We use to go over there a lot until I met this one girl name Toni. Mrs. Watson had cooked some of her 6 inch homemade cakes. They were good, but still not as good as my mama's.

Mrs. Watson sent us kids outside to play while she was cooking. I had never had a bike before so when one of her sons asked me did I want to go for a ride on his bike with him, of course I said yea. He was much older than I was. We went across this little beaver bridge by their house. I called it a beaver bridge because beavers always crossed underneath the bridge. We went up this hill. Before I knew it that bike ride became a nightmare. He stopped the bike and got off. I told him I was ready to go. As I was saying that he grabbed me off the bike and threw me on the ground and pulled down my shorts. No matter how hard I fought him the rougher he got. He held me down and proceeded to rape me. After he was done taking my innocence from me he told me to pull up my shorts. Then he told me I better not tell anyone what he did to me or he would hurt me or another one of my sisters. When we made it back to his house one of my sisters asked me why was I so dirty? I told her we fell of the bike. I was just a kid, and afraid of him, that I never told anyone, until it came back to haunt me. I had suppressed that memory for years. After that day I was afraid to go over there house, but I kept going anyway so no one would ask me questions like why I didn't want to go over there anymore.

Some years later I saw a talk show about women that were raped years earlier and it came back to haunt them. I used to think they were lying until one day my memory of being raped came back to me. I just didn't think it was possible to forget about something that was so terrible in someone's life. Well it triggered my inner being and almost made me feel like my whole world had turned upside down.

I felt like I was going crazy. I was so messed up in the head that I was ready to go and find him and kill him from taking something so precious from me. The sister that I told what had happened to me told me he had gone to prison for the second time for rape and someone killed him in prison. I didn't know what I was feeling at that moment. I knew I was upset that I got cheated out of facing him after what he had done to me.

One day I was riding in the car with one of my brother's and his wife when my brother made a statement that he was gone, so no one will know if he really did those rapes or not, before I knew it I blurted out "he did it" I never knew if he caught on to that or not. I thank God that I no longer let that nightmare control me when it tries to come back at me. I can say that I do finally forgive him with the Lord's help.

It hurt me when I find out someone sexually or any other way hurt a little helpless child. While I was writing this book I shed a lot of tears about all the bad things that has happened to me in my short life time. I tried to focus on my story helping someone else that, I bit the bullet to get this book done. Every time I would think about quitting I had to be strong. It brought out many nightmares, but if it could be some help to someone else I had to finish it. I had to get it done no matter how it was tearing me up inside. I do know one thing, that when I am done with this book I never want to read it again, ever. Thank you Jesus!

Chapter 4

It was a sunny, hot beautiful Wednesday morning in May. My sisters and brothers and I were outside on the porch waiting for our bright yellow school bus to pick us up. There was this really bad boy name Tommy that sat behind me. Tommy was always bullying anyone that was smaller than he was. No one liked him. I used to hate to ride the school bus because of him. One particular day, Tommy was saying mean things to me when I was sitting in my seat minding my own business. Tommy took off his belt and put it around my neck and started to choke me. From that day on, I hated to ride the bus to school. My sisters and brothers were sitting up front. No one knew what was going on until after I got the belt from around my neck. Our school was far from our house, so if you missed the school bus there was no way of getting to school. I use to hide in the back yard until the bus left. Lots of times, then I would come out and get my whooping and go out and play. I never told my parents about what Tommy did.

I even hated to go to school. There was always someone picking on me. My parents had seven girls. I was the only one that had big breasts. All my other sisters had been blessed with the hips and butt. I was self-conscious of how I looked. I never liked the way I looked even to this day. It is very hard for me to buy nice clothes that had that perfect fit and not show so much of my build that I didn't and still don't like.

It was no picnic when I went to school. Kids can be so cruel and they definitely were. People always thought that I just didn't want to go to school. The real reason was because of the way the kids used to treat me. They made me hate going to school and made me hate myself because I had big breasts.

I had one close friend that went to the same school that I went to. Her name was Toni Williams. Toni and her family lived a few miles away from where we lived. Toni had six sisters and two brothers. Toni's mother and my mother were best friends. The town where we lived was made up of mostly hard-working class people that struggled to take care of their families. But, the Williams' seemed to live like they were rich for they would buy nice cars every year. They lived in a big, beautiful home. Toni and her siblings always dressed nice and kept their hair done.

Mrs. Williams was a beautiful lady. She was a teacher at our school. She was a sophisticated and a classy woman. She always walked like she was walking down the runway of a beauty pageant.

Mrs. Williams wore fancy, expensive dresses and pant suits with shoes and hats to match. Her handbags were always matching her clothes. She always smelled nice. She would go out of town to shop for her clothes and shoes.

We had no nice clothing stores in our little town. Mrs. Williams liked to shop at Macy's department store. That was a very nice and expensive store. When she would go to Macy's to buy her perfume, she would tell the salesperson to give her a particular perfume without asking what the price was. Mrs. Williams also wore expensive jewelry. She even got her hair done every Saturday morning. She had her nails done every two weeks. Back then getting nails done was a regular manicure, but now they can put all kinds of designs on them. She always moved with elegance and grace.

Mr. Williams was a man that could bully anyone that was weaker than him. Mr. Williams was a mean man. He was always beating on some of his kids. He was a local policeman. Around town, he was known as the Iceman because he was so cold. He would never smile. He also dressed very nice. He wore fancy suits and shoes to match his clothes as well. He always wore ties with tie clips and cuff links to match. His shoes had to be Stacy Adams or he would not wear them. He wore a lot of jewelry. He even got his hands manicured. They always looked like they were going to a special event.

The Williams' children starting with Renee was twenty-two years old. Renee had moved out of her parents' home when she was nineteen years old. Renee was a beautiful girl. She had long, black, silky hair but she was a very unhappy girl. She got married when she was twenty. Renee always said she was going to get away from her father for some reasons and she did just that.

Kevin was twenty-six. He was the splitting image of his father. He also was a bully just like his father. He always thought he was every woman's dream man. I always thought he was a butt-hole, myself. I didn't care for him much.

Then there was John. He was nineteen. John moved out of his parents' home when he was eighteen. John was a handsome young man. He was very unhappy. Mr. Williams always picked on him for some reason or another. He was very obedient to his parents but Mr. Williams was always so mean to him.

Vanessa was twenty. She had two children and she was eight months pregnant. She was a pretty young lady. She didn't have a problem with her parents. Money was her main reason for not caring about what was going on around her, with her parents and other family members.

Liz was twenty-four. She had four children and was seven months pregnant with her fifth child. Liz is kind of a business woman. If something means getting paid, she was all for it.

Julia was seventeen. She was a straight "A" student. She used to miss a lot of school. I did not understand how she got such good grades. Julia was a pretty young lady. She had short beautiful black hair. She was crazy about her father.

Suzanne was sixteen. She always wore pretty clothes and shoes. Suzanne seemed to have on a new outfit almost every day. She was also a very pretty girl. She was her father's favorite.

Now Toni; she was fourteen. She truly was my friend. She was a very unhappy child. She was pretty. Her hair was silky black and long. She was a petite girl with an hour-glass figure. She wanted to always stay with me at my house for some reason.

Sherry was thirteen. She still liked to play with dolls. She also liked to hang out with her mother. One of her joys was helping her mother in the kitchen. Sherry was not a pretty girl but she was respectable.

Chapter 5

It was a beautiful sunny Saturday. On Saturday's we looked forward to going to the store with our parents. The Williams' kids were going to the store with us too.

We used to be so excited because, we got to ride on the back of daddy's truck. Once again it was time for our parents to make their same old "going to the store on Saturday" speech; "Don't touch "ANYTHING" and absolutely "NO" playing around in the store!" After the public service announcement was made, we piled onto the back of daddy's truck and we were on our way. We were talking loud and playing. Mama shouted, "We are just a mile away from home we can take you back if y'all don't behave." So of course, we lowered our voices. When we got to the store, we were given the same old speech again; "Don't touch ANYTHING" and absolutely "NO" playing around in the store.

When mama and daddy were finished shopping, we were responsible for the loading of the truck at the store and unloading the truck when we made it home. After all the fun and excitement, of our Saturday shopping, mama told us to go outside and play.

We had so much fun when the Williams' kids came over. Mama came outside with milk and cookies. Because there was so much open space, we could see company coming from a long way's away. We saw Mrs. Williams coming to pick up her children.

When I told Toni her mama was coming, she would become very quiet and a sad expression would come across her face. Sherry asked her mom if they could spend the night. Mrs. Williams said she had to ask her husband. Mrs. Williams told her kids to go back outside to play because she was going to stay and visit for a while.

About an hour or so had passed and I looked down the road and saw Mr. Williams coming. When he arrived, Mrs. Williams asked if the kids could spend the night with us. He said yes, but Toni could not stay because she needed to finish cleaning the porch. Mrs. Williams told Mr. Williams that she would finish the work for her. He said to Mrs. Williams, "What did I say?"

After the discussion Mrs. William's went back into the house to tell Toni she couldn't stay because she had to finish cleaning the porch. Toni said mama, "daddy didn't tell me to clean the porch." Mrs. Williams said to her, "I know baby." Toni went and told the other kids she couldn't spend the night. By that time, Mr. Williams came in, he said tomorrow is Sunday we have to go to church. The kids will have to spend the night another time.

The Williams' always went to church. Mr. Williams was a deacon and Mrs. Williams was the accountant at the church. They hardly ever missed a Sunday. They even went to Sunday night services and services during the week.

Most of the girls seemed to be ok until they would see their father. Mr. Williams was so weird, he made my skin crawl. He used to look at us like we were a display at a buffet table. One day, Mr. Williams told Toni to go clean the basement. After about ten minutes, Mr. Williams went into the basement. He told everyone not to come in the basement because he needed to talk to Toni alone.

Mr. Williams told Toni she was going to be punished for not cleaning the basement like he told her to. Toni said, "Daddy, I just didn't hear you when you told me to clean the basement." After that portion of the conversation something seemed quite strange. No one heard anything else. It became very silent in the basement.

After about twenty minutes, Mr. Williams came upstairs. Toni stayed down in the basement. I began to wonder what took him so long to come back upstairs. He looked very strange. I asked if I could go into the basement where Toni was and his reply to me was, "No." She has to finish cleaning the basement all by herself.

About an hour later, Toni came upstairs. She looked like she had been crying. She became very withdrawn. She seemed like she was so sad. I decided to ask Toni why were they so afraid of their father, especially when they were alone with him? Sherry started to say that their father made them do all kinds of weird things. I then asked what kind of weird things? Then, Toni told Sherry to be quiet. She said you know what daddy said so you better shut up, I don't want daddy to find out we were talking about this.

When they said that, it made me more suspicious. I left the subject alone but I kept my eyes on Mr. Williams from that day on. After that day, I started to notice that Mr. Williams was changing towards me. He started to ask me if I wanted anything from the store. He gave me money. He would ask me what kind of cookies and candy I liked. He just started treating me so nice. That was strange because he always acted kind of mean.

Chapter 6

Three weeks had passed since I'd asked Sherry about what she said their father had been doing to them. Sherry always acted like she wanted to tell me something but was afraid to. When I caught Sherry alone I asked her did she remember the conversation we had a few weeks ago. She said yes. I asked her what kind of things she said their father was doing to them? Sherry said he made them sleep with him and their brothers, so they could become pregnant and they could sell the babies. I became speechless.

Sherry said their father even had a few of his friends sleep with them so they could get pregnant. I couldn't believe what I was hearing. I sat back in my chair and didn't say a word for a few minutes. I just couldn't understand why a father would do those things to his kids. My father would have never done those things to us for nothing in the world. I wonder if their brothers were forced to do that to their sisters or if they like having sex with their sisters. Mr. Williams sounded like he was a devil.

I asked Sherry had she let any other grown up know what they were doing to them. She said no. Then she said she didn't want to talk about it anymore. Sherry begged me not to tell anyone what she told me. I told Sherry that someone needed to know what was going on here. She began to cry and said she should not have told me anything.   Now she could be in big trouble. Sherry made me promise not to tell anyone what she had told me. I told her I wouldn't tell anyone, but I didn't like it at all.

It was morning. I smelled bacon and sausage.   Mrs. Williams had cooked breakfast. Mrs. Williams could cook but still not as good as my mama could. We ate and afterward went for a walk. I wanted to know if Mrs. Williams knew about what was going on with her children.

I hated to think that a mother would allow this to happen to her girls. I started to watch Mrs. Williams's every move. I wanted to know if she knew.   From what I saw, she had to know. She was allowing her daughters to sleep with her husband, their father and brothers. It was so unthinkable. I had never heard anything like that before. Now I know why he had looked at me in such a strange way.

I started to think about the times the girls wouldn't come to school.   It wasn't just a sick day or a skip day. It was for a few months sometimes, and they still got passing grades. I just could not understand that at all. I asked Toni and Sherry to tell me everything. Toni was still reluctant to talk. I had to get Sherry away by herself.

When I asked Sherry about what she said before, she just told me to forget everything, because she was afraid. She said her dad told them if they said anything about what was going on, they would also be in trouble, because they were helping them with the business.

He had them so intimidated that they really thought they would be in trouble. I told Sherry they wouldn't be in trouble, because they were kids. I couldn't convince her that they wouldn't be in trouble. I decided to leave it alone.

Mr. and Mrs. Williams had their children brainwashed, and for years, that's why their secrets were so well kept, and some got paid to keep the secret.

I started to spend the night with Toni more often. I wanted to observe Mr. and Mrs. Williams, so I could find out even more about what they were doing. I thought that if I spent the night over Toni's more often that maybe they wouldn't bother the girls. Well that didn't matter much, because they continued to have sex with them. Mr. Williams continued buying me things like candy and perfume. I asked him why? He replied I heard you telling Toni you didn't have any. Then I thanked him.

I would stay over to the Williams house a lot because Toni was my best friend, and what Mr. Williams friends was doing to them maybe some days they wouldn't touch them.

If mama ever were to find out what Mr. Williams and his sons were doing to those girls, I would never be able to stay the night again. If my father found out what his old friend was doing to his own daughters he would probably kill him.

I didn't know what to do. Should I have told someone or just left it alone for then? I didn't know. I just waited and gave it some thought.

It was time for me to go home. I was always over the Williams house. Sometimes I would spend the night during the week. But most of the time I would spend the night during the weekend. When I did spend the night on a weekday I would ride the bus with Toni, and her sisters and brothers. When I got to school that morning, Sherry became sick. She had vomited all down the hall. I took her to see the school nurse. They called her parents. The principle told them they needed to come and pick her up. Mr. Williams said he wasn't. "She's okay"! Mr. Williams said she just wants some attention. They made her stay at the school the rest of that day.

The weekend came, I couldn't wait to get home to get some clothes and go over to Toni's house. I found myself wanting to spend the night often. I started to like the presents Mr. Williams were giving me. His wife had also started to buy me things. Things I had never had before because my parents couldn't afford it. I just loved it. I liked it so much that I started to ask for things. I would say to Mr. Williams "I wish I had a new pair of shoes." He would ask me what kind of shoes? I would say a pair of gym shoes. He said he would buy me a new pair of shoes. I knew Mr. Williams was going to buy them. I was able to go to the store during the week. So I stayed with the Williams more often during the week. Mr. and Mrs. Williams's were going to the store tomorrow. I wanted to make sure I was there so Mr. Williams could buy me something.

It was Saturday morning and time for us to go to the store. Mrs. Williams asked me if I want a new dress to wear to church the next day. I said yes. We went to Macy's department store. That was the first time I ever got to go to any expensive clothing store. My parents could not afford to take us shopping, so we had to wear hand me down clothes. You could just imagine how I felt.

I just couldn't believe that I was in an expensive store. There were dresses that cost over five hundred dollars. Mrs. Williams told me to pick the dress I liked. I started to look at the cheapest dresses. I didn't like any of the cheaper ones. I finally found a dress I liked. It cost three hundred and fifty dollars. Mrs. Williams bought it for me.

We had made it to the shoe store. I was looking at all the nice selection of shoes they had. It took a while for me to find some shoes I liked. When I did find them they cost one hundred and twenty five dollars. I just couldn't believe I had clothes that came from Macys. It felt like Christmas, not the Christmas I remember when I was just getting candy and nuts.

When we made it back to the house, I went to Toni's room to show her what her mom and dad bought me. About an hour later Mr. Williams asked me to put my dress on so he could see how it fit. I felt a little strange. I put it on anyway. He told me to turn around so he could see me. At that moment a funny feeling came over me. I felt very uncomfortable. I felt dirty.

I needed a bath. It was time to get ready for bed. I had an early start the next morning for Sunday school at church.

Mrs. Williams woke us all up so we could get ready for church. I started to get dressed. And I just couldn't believe I had a new dress. I took my time getting dressed because I wanted everything to look good.

Everyone was ready to get into the cars and get going. Mr. Williams told me to ride along in the car with him. I didn't want to but I did anyway. At church the service was very good, but I couldn't stop myself from thinking about what Mr. Williams was doing to his daughters. I wanted to tell someone, but getting such nice things was stopping me from telling anyone anything.

It was Sunday night. Everything seemed to be going so well. We all were sitting in the living room eating popcorn and drinking soda. We were watching television while the food was cooking.

Mr. Williams went upstairs. A few minutes later he called for Toni. The expression on her face was terrifying. About twenty minutes later like the other times, it was like clockwork, Mr. Williams came down stairs, but Toni didn't. I wanted to go up there but I was afraid to. I thought that if I did Mr. Williams would be mad. I had begun to wonder why Toni still didn't come from upstairs for an hour.

Mrs. Williams was on her way up the stairs when Mr. Williams told her to send Toni down to help her with dinner. Okay she replied. It always seemed like Toni was always doing more work than anyone else. I hardly ever saw any of the other children doing anything.

When Mrs. Williams got up the stairs she noticed Toni lying on their bed with her clothes half off. She called Toni's name, there was no answer. So she went over and shook her. And still no answer. She stormed back down the stairs shouting to Mr. Williams. "There's something wrong with Toni!" She screamed. "Call an ambulance, she's not waking up!" Mr. Williams was taking his time. After a little while Mr. Williams decided to call an ambulance.

It was going to take a while. The Williams house was kind of far from any emergency services. I waited for the ambulance at the front door. After a few minutes I started to hear the sirens getting closer. When they arrived I told them to go up stairs. The paramedics had all their emergency tools in a small black bag. They checked all of Toni's vital signs and they all seemed to be normal. They asked her mother was she on any kind of medication? "No" she said, they also asked about street drugs but the answer was still no. At the time I didn't know what street drugs were. "Later I would find out in a big way." The paramedics seemed to still be wondering about drugs that Toni could have gotten into. They told Mrs. Williams that Toni seemed to be asleep. So Mrs. Williams said she had had some type of sleeping pills. She said there were only two left in the bottle and they were gone.

The paramedics put Toni on a stretcher to take her to the hospital. They also told us that if she had only took two sleeping pills that she would be okay. Mr. Williams panicked and said, "you might as well leave her home to sleep it off instead of taking her all the way to the hospital". The paramedics said they would be in trouble if they didn't take her to the hospital. They were not 100% sure about what was wrong with her.

The paramedics were on their way to the hospital. Mr. and Mrs. Williams let me ride in the ambulance with Toni. They followed the ambulance to St. Joseph hospital. Mr. Williams told Sherry to watch the house. When they got there, the receptionist told the Williams to sign papers for treatment and billing.

Two hours had passed since they had arrived. The doctor then came out and started asking the Williams questions. Like where the bruises came from that were on Toni's body. Mr. Williams said that Toni was in a fight with another girl that stayed down the street. He said it had happened a few days ago. The doctor responded by saying that the bruises' were fresh. The doctor said Toni had bite marks in the inner thigh on her left side. The doctor said smartly that "when young girls fight, they don't usually bite another girl in the inner thigh". He also told them that he was going to perform a pap-smear. They also were going to run some blood test on Toni. The Williams seemed kind of nervous. It seemed to be taking a long time.

The doctor said that he would be calling child protective services and they had suspected child abuse. Mr. Williams seemed very nervous. He told the doctor he was taking Toni home. The doctors asked Mr. Williams if he wanted to find out why Toni had the bruises. I told you she got into a fight! "He shouted." The child

Investigation Services would like to have a meeting with you in the conference room. They began by asking questions like if Toni had a boyfriend. No they said. The child protective service told the Williams' that Toni was two months pregnant. They said they were waiting for Toni to wake up so they could interview her not only about the baby's father but about the bruises. Mr. Williams face became flushed. He said he was going to take Toni home. The investigator said that if they didn't let them interview her now that they would be coming to his home. The Williams' started to put Toni's clothes back on. She was awake but she didn't know what was going on at all.

They rushed to get Toni out of the hospital. When they dressed her we rushed out the door. The guard shouted for us to stop. We all got in the car and drove off.

When we returned home Mr. Williams made sure to tell everyone not to answer the door or the phone. He had become so nervous he couldn't eat. The following day no one showed up. After a few days still no one showed up. They never came.

Sadly enough Mr. Williams got comfortable with himself. He was back to his old ways. Mrs. Williams wanted them to stay low for a while. Mr. Williams however didn't want to hear that. So they were back to business as usual.

Chapter 7

I was in the basement with Toni. She looked very strange. I asked her what was wrong. She asked if she could tell me something that was going on with her daddy and mama. She asked me not to tell anyone about anything she was going to tell me. I said whatever she tells me I would keep it a secret. She began by telling me that her daddy and brothers had made her have sex with them so she could become pregnant. They wanted to sell the babies to other people. My eyes opened as wide as they could. I asked her how long has this been going on? She told me ever since us girls had gotten our first period. I asked about the others. She said that all of the sisters have had a baby but Sherry, but she was pregnant now. Mama and daddy just sold them for ten thousand dollars or more each, Toni said. There goes my mouth again opening as wide as a jokers smile. I wanted to know if this was real or was I dreaming. I had never heard of anything like that before. She continued by telling me about the child she had had at thirteen years old and the one that she is presently carrying.

I asked if she had told an adult or anyone else about this. She told me no. I asked why not? She said that if she told anyone her parents said that the state would take them away. Then her parents said that they would live with people that would do all kinds of things to them. I had heard this same thing from Sherry, but it was still surprising to hear. Suzanne had had two children. She is daddy's favorite Toni said. Toni also said that Suzanne would do anything her daddy told her to do. She said Suzanne loves having babies for daddy because she knows she can have anything she ask daddy for. And if I had something and Suzanne wanted it daddy made me give it to her. Suzanne loved money just like her parents. As long as daddy kept buying her things she would keep having babies for them, Toni said. He takes her to the stores and buys her whatever she wants.

Julia had two babies. But Mr. Williams had not slept with her. John had been sleeping with Julia and me, Toni said. That's why he moved out of the house so young. He hated his parents for making him have sex with his sisters.

Renee was sleeping with daddy and Kevin. She had four kids. She didn't know who their fathers were. Kevin, John, or my daddy could have been those babies daddy Toni said. I guess it didn't matter really because they were selling the babies any way. It was ok as long as she was getting paid well. Renee didn't like regular jobs because she was being paid well for having babies for her parents.

Toni went on to say that they were not the only ones having babies for her parents. I asked Toni what she meant they are not the only ones. Toni said that there were a few girls at her school that were having babies with their daddy. Toni said her mother was a teacher so she can recruit some of the girls by going through their files. Toni said her mama always knew what kind of girls would do this or not. She peeps out the girls that wear the same clothes all the time. She even looks at the ones that don't have their hair fixed all the time. Toni said her mama figured those were poor people that will do anything for some extra money. I asked Toni what she got for having these babies for her parents. Toni said her daddy said that they are taking care of them with food and clothes and keeping their hair done, and whatever else they need, so they don't have to pay them.

I had to be careful how to ask Toni these questions because she was already nervous about telling me anything. I asked Toni what about when it's time for the babies to be born, because I didn't think they could go to the hospital because this is illegal. She said her mama and daddy has a hired registered nurse that they knew at the hospital that delivers the babies when she doesn't have to work at the hospital. Her name was Mrs. Jane.

Toni told me that if something goes wrong and a baby dies they just bury them in the back yard. I asked her are there any babies buried in the back yard now? Toni said there are two babies buried out back. When Toni told me about the babies that were buried in the back yard I became very nervous. I was afraid of dead people. I had to pretend it didn't mean much to me so she doesn't think I was going to tell anyone.

I needed to dig deeper so I asked Toni where the babies were delivered. She said they had a room in the basement that was set up like a real doctor's office. Toni said it has a bed with stirrups and all the necessary things they need to deliver the babies. She said they even have a medicine cabinet that was always locked. I asked Toni could I go down stairs to see the delivery room. She said she will take me down there when her mama and daddy go someplace and will be gone a long time.

Toni started to tell me that her mama gets to open files on any student at the school because she is an English teacher at the same school we go to. Toni said when her mother sees a potential candidate for their illegal baby selling scam she does research on them. She used school records. Mrs. Williams even investigated the girl's family. They want to focus on the poorest families that might do just about anything for some extra money.

The Williams' seem to have the town locked up in this illegal business. They had the help of the principal, and the local police are also paid off to keep quiet. Even the preacher has heard about this business, but he chooses to ignore it as long as the Williams keep paying their 10% percent tithes and hefty offerings, he just swept it under the pulpit.

Mrs. Williams does the book-keeping on the family business and also the book keeping at the church. The Williams has all kinds of records on the girls and the customers. Now I know why the girls were getting good grades after missing so much school. The principal alters the attendant's records. It almost seemed like the perfect scam.

Chapter 8

It was a hot muggy Wednesday morning. This was the week of parents and teachers conferences. Both of Toni's parents had to go to the school. They had to be there at ten o'clock that morning. I was still at the Williams house because we didn't have school that day. As soon as Mr. and Mrs. Williams pulled out the drive way Toni and I rushed to the basement, so I could see the room that they deliver the babies in. The door was locked but Toni knew where the keys were. Toni opened the door to the room. The room did look just like a real delivery room. I was afraid to be in there because I didn't know if Toni's parents would have to double back for anything and catch us in that room. Toni reassured me that her parents would be gone for a few hours.

I was amazed at what I was looking at. It all seems like a bad dream that I was going to wake up from soon. I knew it was not a dream. I finally saw everything Toni was telling me was true. I asked Toni what she was going to do about all this. She said she was not going to do anything because all of them would be in trouble. Toni went on to say she didn't care about herself much but she didn't want her parents to be in any trouble. Toni had been brainwashed good. Toni really did think she was going to be in trouble if she told anyone about what her parents was having her do. I could not convince her that she would not be in any trouble because she was a child. So I decided to just leave that alone before she stopped telling me anything. I just stopped that line of questioning all together.

Toni asked me about what I would do if her parents asked me if I wanted to work for them. I looked at Toni and said they wouldn't ask me anything like that. When Toni asked me that, I began to feel like I was being bought. I started to think about all the nice things Mr. and Mrs. Williams was buying me. I put two and two together and thought that's why they have been so nice to me lately. They were buttering me up for the slaughter.

Being a poor little school girl that had not been able to have such nice things because her parents were hard working tax payers trying to stay above water couldn't afford such beautiful things. I just couldn't stop thinking about the way Toni and her family was living such a life. I thank God; I would rather have had love in my family than a cold dark and lonely existing. I felt so bad for Toni and her sisters. I had become so uncomfortable when I was over the Williams house.

I decided to take advantage of the nice things I was getting. I said I would just get what I could until that played out.

I was always waiting for the conversation about me being employed in the family business. I knew it was getting closer and closer each day. I was on pins and needles waiting for the shoe to drop. So in the mean time I used it to my advantage until the big day.

I started to ask could they get my hair and nails done any chance I got. I still couldn't believe that they were going to ask me about having babies for them to sell. Toni said they would ask and it would be very soon. I asked Toni why she would say something like that. Toni said because her parents were talking about it a few days ago. I said for Toni to stop playing. She said she wasn't playing. I told her I don't know what I would say. Toni made me promise again that I wouldn't say anything about all of this she was telling me.

A part of me wanted to tell someone about this but I didn't want Toni to be in any trouble for telling me everything. I promised Toni again that I wouldn't tell anyone about the business. The reason I promised was so she could keep telling me everything.

I was very young back then. I didn't know what to do. I couldn't talk to anyone about it because I promised Toni I wouldn't. It seemed as if I was in the middle of two lions being pulled in two directions. All I could do was keep quiet. That was a lot to carry being a kid myself.

Mr. and Mrs. Williams were back from the school. We had already gone back up the stairs. Mrs. Williams started to cook dinner. She was cooking some spaghetti with lots of sauce and meat, just the way I like it. She was also frying some catfish and garlic toast and making a salad. Mrs. Williams asked me what my favorite dessert was. I told her German chocolate cake. I really had lots of favorites, but I had a craving for German Chocolate cakes.

Chapter 9

A few weeks had gone past and it was almost time for summer break. I was back at home with my family. I have not seen Toni for a whole week. It was now the weekend. I asked my parents could I spend the night with Toni. They said it was ok with them, but Toni had to ask her parents if it was ok. I knew they would say yes. So I packed my things and mama took me over to the Williams house. Everyone was there. Mama and Mrs. Williams were having coffee at the kitchen table. It was a hot Saturday morning. I loved being over the Williams house on Saturdays because they always went out of town to shop.

I had gotten use to having new clothes and shoes, perfume and make-up. I really did miss going to the store with my family. I just couldn't trade new clothes and shoes for some cookies and candy. I guess I did forget where I came from.

Mama got her things and went home. Mrs. Williams called for me to come upstairs. She wanted to show me all the nice things she had. Mrs. Williams started to talk about how I would like to be able to have such nice things in my closet. I thought to myself first I had to get a closet because we didn't have any in our house. I said that would be nice to have some boots like those there. Mrs. Williams said well lets go to the store to see if they still had the same ones.

We all piled up in the car. We drove about forty five minutes to a store called the Classy Woman's Boutique. Mrs. Williams, me, Toni, Suzanne and Sherry all went. Sherry was eight months pregnant. It didn't look like she was no more than four months.

Suzanne always looked good even when she was pregnant. I didn't like her much because she thought she was the best looking girl in town. Suzanne was seven months pregnant. I just plain couldn't stand her. Suzanne couldn't do anything wrong in her father's eyes.

We all got out the car and went into the boutique. They had the most beautiful expensive clothes I had ever seen. This place was even more elegant than Macy's. Their shoes looked like they were almost too elegant to wear. I felt like I was dreaming. This boutique looked like you had to have an appointment to get in.

We all looked around to see all the beautiful clothes. I went into the shoe department as always. The prices on the shoes were ridiculous. It was like making a house note.

I saw a pair of beautiful black leather shoes. I could not wait another minute to try them on. I had to go over to see if they had a pair in my size. I asked the saleswoman if they had a size 7. She said yes. Then she asked me if I wanted to try them on? I said yes please.

The saleswoman went into the back to get the shoes. When she got back, she helped me take my shoes off. Then she put nylon footie's on my feet. I had never heard of a store providing stockings to customers free of charge, actually I had never heard of any stores that even provide footie's for a price, just to try on shoes.

The lady helped me put the shoes on. I fell in love with those boots when I first saw them on my feet. Then I looked at the price. They cost two hundred dollars. I admired them for about five minutes, and then I took them off and gave them back to the saleswoman. Toni asked why I gave them back. I said they cost too much money. Toni said so and went over to her mother and told her that I liked a pair of shoes but I thought they cost too much money. Mrs. Williams asked Toni if I really wanted the shoes and if I did to tell me I could get them. I had gone to the store with the Williams' before and they bought me some expensive shoes and dresses before, but I really did like those shoes better than anything else I had gotten. Mrs. Williams bought them for me.

I was very happy, but all of a sudden a light turned on in my head. I had to remind myself about how I was going to explain all these beautiful things I was getting to my parents. The things were not from goodwill or anyplace like that. I didn't put too much thought into it as long as I got those shoes.

We were done shopping and on our way home. I had started to think about if this was going to be the day that Toni's parents was going to ask me the one million dollar question. The shoes quickly slipped out of my mind as soon as I thought about the Williams' asking me the big question. I would be happy when they asked me, so I could breathe again.

I was rehearsing in my mind what I might say when they approached me. When we got back to the house Toni and I took our things into the house and went in the back yard. Toni wanted to know what I was going to say when her parents ask me the question. I told her I didn't know what I was going to say and that I wish they would get it over with. Toni also asked me if I really liked those things her parents were buying me. I said yes. Then she said that if I do it I will have my own money to buy my own things.

Toni's parents called her in the house so they could talk to her alone. Toni went in the house. After about fifteen minutes Toni came back outside, and then she said I can stop wondering when they were going to ask me the question. I asked her why? She said they are going to call me in the house in a few minutes to ask me. I told Toni to stop playing, she said she was serious. I began to sweat profusely. I didn't know how to calm down, but I knew I had to get it together before they call me in to ask me. Without them getting suspicious about me already knowing what they were going to ask me.

About fifteen minutes later Mrs. Williams asked me could she talk to me for a minute, I said yes and I will be in a few minutes. Mrs. Williams went back into the house. Toni said please; don't forget you promised me you will not let them know that I told you anything. I told Toni not to worry, I promised I wouldn't tell and I want.

It was now time for me to go in the house. I was so nervous that I was sweating bullets. It felt like I was going to faint. I had to find a way to compose myself before I went in the house. As I opened the door I looked in Mr. and Mrs. Williams face. They were sitting at the kitchen table. They both were drinking coffee. Mrs. Williams was sitting at the head of the table drinking coffee out of a tea cup with her pinky finger sticking out.

Mr. Williams asked me to have a seat. I tried to be as calm as possible. I asked them did I do anything wrong? Just to try and throw them off. They said no, that they just needed to talk to me about something. I said ok. I sat down at the table. Mrs. Williams asked me did I like all those gifts they had been giving me. I said yes. Then she continued with would I like to be able to buy those things myself. I said yes. She asked me would I like to know how? I said yes. Then she started to say I know you noticed that our daughters are always pregnant? I said yes again. She asked me have I ever seen any babies in the house. I said no. Mrs. Williams started saying that they don't have any babies in the house because when the babies are born they sell them to those people who couldn't have any children. I said I don't understand I had to make it look good. Mr. Williams went on to try and throw a guilt trip on me, by saying would you like to help a woman that is not able to have kids of her own. I said I guess so. He went on to say it is so sad that a couple can't have any children of their own. He went on to say, I can help them by giving them a family and make a lot of money at the same time.

Mrs. Williams started by saying all I have to do is get pregnant and when I have the baby we will just sell the baby to a poor couple that can't have kids. "Isn't that a nice thing to do?" Mrs. Williams asked. I said yes I guess so. Then I asked how much money would I get? Mr. Williams said they we will pay me fifteen hundred dollars. Being so young and naive I saw dollar signs shoes and dresses.

They convinced me that I was just doing a good deed for people that couldn't carry their name on. Even if it was not their blood kin, no one would know they said. How much more can you do for a person? Mrs. Williams asked. I didn't respond. They were laying it on thick. I didn't know any difference. I was only fourteen years old at that time. So I was convinced that I would be doing a good deed.

I wanted to know how I would have a baby when I didn't have a boyfriend. I was saying that so they wouldn't think I knew what they were doing to their daughters? Mr. Williams says he or his son Kevin will have sex with me and get me pregnant. I looked at Mrs. Williams to see if she was going to have any kind of reaction when her husband said he will get me pregnant. She says to me it's ok because it is doing mankind a good deed. I didn't know how to take that so I didn't say anything. They told me it had to be a secret because, other people are so cruel that they will try to put us in jail for doing the best thing we can for other people.

I had to think long and hard about how was I going to pull this off. How was I supposed to keep this entire secret from my family? Mr. and Mrs. Williams said they will figure out everything and just for me not to worry. They said they will let me know when it's time to get started.

After they were done talking to me I went back outside where Toni was. I looked at Toni and she gave me a look of suspense. Toni said did they ask me the million dollar question? I said, yes they did. Toni responded with "what did you say?" I said to Toni I said yes. Toni was getting on my nerves asking me questions. Then she said are you really sure you want to do it? I said to Toni, just stop asking me the same question, I said yes and don't ask me again.

Toni had pissed me off. I said to her I will be helping people that can't have kids on their own and get paid for it at the same time.

Toni said now you understand why I can't say anything about what was going on. Both of us were only fourteen years old. We didn't question too much of what was going on. I found out much later that I had been brainwashed just like Toni was.

Chapter 10

It was still summer time, and we were still out on our summer break. A week after school was out. I had gone home to spend some time with my own family. Mama and daddy didn't mind me staying over at Toni's house a lot because I always came back with a lot of beautiful clothes that my sisters could wear. We were out for summer break so I got to be at Toni's house even more.

I was getting ready to go back over The Williams' house when mama asked me a question that took me by surprise. Mama asked me why Mr. and Mrs. Williams were buying me all those nice things. I didn't know what to say, but I knew I had to think of something quick. I said to mama that when we go to the store on Saturdays that the Williams must didn't want me to be left out. I said to mama isn't that nice? Mama said it sure is. I got past that question now I could breathe again.

I was on my way back over the Williams' house. When I got there it felt like I was over there for the first time. My palms were sweaty and I was very nervous. I had to calm down before I had a nervous breakdown. I had to calm my nervous before anyone saw me. I walked in like I had always, but I was on pins and needles with sweaty palms. All night long I was waiting for Kevin or his father to approach me about having sex with them. The whole night had come and went without anyone saying anything to me. A few days had gone past without a word. Then on a Monday night we all were sitting around the television watching a western when Mr. Williams asked was I ready to get started? I looked at Mrs. Williams; she noticed I was hesitant so she told me it was ok. So we went upstairs, Mr. Williams and me. When we got to the bedroom I began to tremble like a leaf blowing in the dusty wind. He said don't be nervous. I said ok. Mr. Williams told me to sit down on the bed. He started to rub me on my back. He slowly removed my blouse. He started to kiss me on my neck, at first it tickled. I gave a little giggle.

Mr. Williams began to take off his shirt. Then he took off his pants. I started to pull down my pants. Mr. Williams started to turn the covers down and told me to lie down beside him, so I did. He started to message my back. It felt real good. He began to turn me over on my back and began to kiss my breasts. He went down to my belly button. He just kept going down and down, until he couldn't go any lower unless he was going to kiss my toes. I didn't understand why he was kissing me on my whole body, but it did feel good. Then he came back up and began to have sex with me. At first I didn't like it much, but after a while it started to feel good, very good. I didn't want him to stop. Something in the back of my mind was telling me this was just plain wrong. After about twenty minutes Mr. Williams was done. We took a shower and went back down the stairs. I felt very strange coming down stairs when I knew everyone else knew what we had just done. After sleeping with Mr. Williams, I started to think about when was the next time we were going to have sex again because I really liked it

I was young so I didn't really know what love making was all about. Anyway whatever it was it sure did feel good. I knew I wanted more and quick.

Mrs. Williams was in the kitchen like always. I asked her if I could talk to her. She said yes. I sat down at the table. I said to Mrs. Williams when do we know if I am pregnant or not? She said after about a few months we will be able to tell if I was pregnant. They didn't have those instant pregnancy tests like they do now. I didn't know much about all this after all I was just fourteen years old and about to turn fifteen, so was Toni.

A few weeks had gone past. Mr. Williams and I had had sex a few more times. I was enjoying it more and more each time. I began to think about him all the time. It was more than having a baby to me now. I was falling for Mr. Williams. I started to put too much time into Mr. Williams than the business deal. I found myself day dreaming about him all the time. I began to ask him to sleep with me all the time. A lot of the time he said he was busy, that hurt my feelings. It was not suppose to be this way. I thought we were to just have sex and that was it. I didn't think of all these feelings were going to come along with making a baby.

Chapter 11

Two months had gone past. My stomach was beginning to get big. I hadn't had a period in two months. I told Mrs. Williams that I hadn't had one. She said I had to be pregnant. I didn't know what to say. I was a little happy just to be having Mr. Williams baby, even if it was going to be sold. After telling everyone I was pregnant they didn't seem to care. Even Mr. Williams was ignoring me. I asked him when we were going to be together again. He said we are not because I was already pregnant. I said I didn't understand. He said there was no need for us to have an affair. I asked him what he meant. He said if we were to sleep together now it would be having an affair. I asked him wasn't we having an affair? He said if it wasn't for business purposes it would be an affair.

I asked Mr. Williams if we could sneak and have an affair. He said yes. I was as happy as a whore on Broadway on the first and third of the month. He said everybody else was going to be at church. I was counting down the hours for them to go. It was three in the afternoon and church didn't start until seven in the evening.

So I was waiting and waiting and waiting. I started to put on red nail and toe polish. I made sure my hair was looking good. I took a long bubble bath. When I was done I put baby oil all over my body.

Men love it when a woman is slick and shiny with oil. Then I put on a pretty red dress.

I had waited for awhile to be with Mr. Williams that I was not about to wait any longer preparing myself when everyone leaves. I want to be ready to get started as soon as possible. I had made all the necessary preparations ahead of time. I wanted to jump on him as soon as everyone went out the door.

Mrs. Williams shouted to whoever was not in the car, "if y'all don't hurry I am going to leave without y'all." I started to shout, "Mrs. Williams says come on "now."

I didn't want anyone in the house with us. As the last person got into the car I shut the door tightly. I ran upstairs and got in the bed. After about ten minutes Mr. Williams came upstairs. He started to take off his clothes. He got in the bed and started to kiss me on my neck. He was so good I didn't want him to stop, ever.

When he was done licking me from head to toe he began to make love to me passionately. It felt so good I wanted to scream. I felt like I was going to explode. When we were done we took a shower and went down stairs to talk. I asked Mr. Williams was he happy about him and I having a baby together? Mr. Williams gave me the strangest look. Then he said us having a baby was business. I just said ok then and began to look at TV. I was not about to let anyone not even him ruin my good feeling.

It was 9:45 at night. Mrs. Williams was parking the car. I was sitting in the living room watching TV. Mr. Williams was in the basement. When Mrs. Williams came in the house, she asked where Willie was at. Mr. Williams' first name was Willie. Mrs. Williams name was Sharon Elizabeth Williams. We were not allowed to call adults by their first name, unless it was Mr. or Mrs. before it. I told her he was in the basement.

It was in the first week of July when I was told I was Pregnant. That mean I was going to have my baby in April. It seemed so far away. Since I had been pregnant I was going to have a hard time being alone with Mr. Williams. The last time Mr. Williams and

I were together he made me feel bad by saying it was just business between us.

I was beginning to think about how I was going to get past Willie treating me like an employee instead of a sex partner. The more I thought about it the more I got angry. I knew it was just a business deal, but I still felt like I was being used.

When I got a chance to be alone with Willie again, I asked him when we were going to make love again. He looked at me and said we can't be together any more until after I have the baby to get me pregnant again. He said he told me that before. I said I know, but why can't we when no one is around? Mr. Williams said no, it's just too much trouble. I became very angry. I told him I hate him and when I have this baby he will never touch me again. I was not about to go for that. I then stormed out the door. After I calmed down and started to think rationally, I needed to do something that would make him make love to me again.

It was Sunday Morning. I went to church with my family. The church service was very moving. Pastor was teaching on the importance of tithes to keep the church house in order. I loved to go to church.

I always felt bad about not having money sometimes. I know I had to pay my tithes I had to get better about paying. Our family gave what they could but the Williams were able to give big financial gifts. Our high school principal went to the same church we belonged to, his name was Mr. Hatcher.

I used to wonder why our principal was coming over to the Williams' house a lot. He never was over there long at all. Mr. Williams was always giving Mr. Hatcher an envelope every time he came over. I didn't find out why until later.

When the church was out I went home to pack some clothes for me to go over the Williams' house. Mr. Williams was going to take me to his house since he was already over there. I was going to be riding in the car with just him and nobody else.

I had a chance to ask Mr. Williams how I was going to keep this pregnancy a secret from my family. Mr. Williams said that he would. He had stated that he had been doing this type of business for years. He told me that if I do as he says that they would never find out that I was pregnant.

He goes on to say that I'm a little thick, so all I'll have to do is keep wearing those big shirts and everything will be ok. For a minute I felt a little embarrassed that he would make a comment about my weight, but he did. I felted like he was calling me a big pig. I said ok.

We were pulling up in the front yard. Mrs. Williams was sitting in the living room reading the Sunday newspaper. Our newspaper was very interesting, because we lived in such a small town that when anything happened to anyone in our town it was put into the newspaper. Mr. Williams said there is going to be a lot of yard sales in the rich white folk neighborhood all week long.

Mrs. Williams asked us do we want to go with her. If we did want to go we had to be up and ready by six o'clock so that we could get the good stuff before it is all taken by others. All of the girls said they will go with her. I told them I didn't like to go to yard sales because they were boring. I had lied to them; I really liked going yard selling. I just wanted a chance to be alone with Mr. Williams. I wanted Mr. Williams and me to have some time alone.

I wanted Mr. Williams to make love to me. Monday morning they were getting ready to go to the yard sales. It seemed like they were taking forever to leave. I guess it just seemed like that because I just wanted them to be gone.

When they piled up in the car I watched them drive off. "Thank you", I said to myself. I quickly showered. I put on some baby oil. I brushed my teeth in a hurry. I felt like I was already wasting time. Mr. Williams was still in bed. When I finished I went into the bedroom where Mr. Williams was still sleeping. I just looked at him for a few minutes.

Then I got into the bed and took off my robe. I kissed him on his forehead. When he woke up he asked me where everyone was. I told him they went yard selling. He looked at me with those bedroom eyes. Those eyes could have gotten him the world, at least a few women. It sure did get me with a little help from his love making.

Mr. Williams began to kiss me on the forehead. He started to caress my breast. He sucked my breast like it was his only source of milk. It felt so good I thought I would faint before he got to the lower part of my body. When he started to stick his tongue in my belly button it seemed like he was there forever maybe because I wanted him to go down further. It just dawn on me you don't have to do all of that to make a baby. I didn't think of that before. Don't get me wrong, I was not complaining, but that had me puzzled. Mr. Williams was just a freak. I wondered did Mrs. Williams know he was doing that. Anyway, I wanted him so bad and for a long time that I felt like I was going to go crazy with anticipation.

When he got to the next level I thought I was going to pass out. Mr. Williams made love to me like I was the best he ever had. When we finished making love he held me in his arms and kissed me. I didn't want it to end, but I knew I had to get out of the bed before Mrs. Williams and the girls got back.

It was now Monday evening we were all sitting around the dinner table talking about what we were going to do the rest of the evening. My mind was stuck on Mr. Williams from earlier when he was making good passionate love to me.

Chapter 12

When school was in, there was not much time to waste. We had homework to keep our mind occupied for awhile. But my mind was still stuck on Mr. Williams and how he knew how to make a girl feel very good. I tried to focus on other things but my mind just wouldn't get off of Mr. Williams.

Toni and I would go for walks to the levee. We use to catch crawdads so we could cook them. We loved to fish. Toni was afraid of worms, so I had to put them on her hook. I used to hate to put worms on someone's hook when I was trying to fish myself. I used to love to eat catfish. Toni liked to fish but she didn't like to eat fish. We would fish for hours. The time would fly by when we were out fishing. It was time for us to be getting back home. When we made it back home it was kind of noisy. We didn't know what was going on. We heard screaming in the house.

When we went inside we asked what was going on. Julia said Sherry was having her baby. Mr. and Mrs. Williams were in the basement with her. They were trying to locate Mrs. Jane the registered nurse they had hired. Mrs. Williams told me to keep trying to call her. About ten minutes later Mrs. Jane was pulling up in the yard. What a relief. She rushed down the basement stairs.

Mrs. Jane made it just in time for Sherry to have her baby. About fifteen minutes later Mr. and Mrs. Williams came up stairs and said Sherry had a baby boy. Suzanne will be the next to deliver her baby. Suzanne was over seven months pregnant. I was about twelve weeks pregnant then. I had a long way to go. Toni was having her baby in January.

Toni said she hates her brother Kevin and her daddy. Toni said she hates it when they touch her. She said it didn't feel right when her father and brother touched her. I told her it didn't suppose to feel right when it's her daddy and brother that's touching her. I wished there were some way I could stop them from touching her.

I asked Toni have she ever told her parents about not wanting to do that anymore? Toni said yes, but it doesn't do any good. I don't think there was a way of telling anyone without them getting in trouble. Sometimes Toni became so sad. I would sometimes cry for her. I knew it had to be terrible to have her own family doing those things to her. The other girls don't seem to think much about it; at least they don't show it as much as Toni does.

I made a choice to be in the family business. I am falling in love with Toni's daddy. I know that was such a nasty thing to do. I am supposed to be her friend and now I am in love with her daddy. I'm quite sure she didn't want me to fall in love with her daddy. What a friend to have. I was anticipating the next time Mr. Williams and I could be together again. That was all I was thinking about.

All of a sudden my imagination started to run away with me. I was thinking that Sherry had just had her baby and now how long will it be until Willie starts to sleep with her again. I could not help but to be jealous. I was young, but I think I knew what being in love felt like. I knew it was wrong but I just couldn't help myself. Even though I was young I still knew what was right and wrong. I think he was falling in love with me too.

It was Wednesday; I was looking out the window when I saw our principal outside talking to Mr. Williams. Like always Mr. Williams handed him an envelope. I knew the principle was shady.

I could only think that those envelopes had money in them. On one particular day I decided to ask Toni about Mr. Hatcher coming over to the house to pick up an envelope from her daddy.

Toni said Mr. Hatcher helps with the business. I asked Toni what she meant. She said that our principal helps with the business by finding some of the girls for the business, and that he gets paid a percentage to make sure the girls gets passing grades. He altered their attendant's records.

Toni said that the local police department is in on the business to keep quiet. So I said the Williams got the police department, the principal, and the teachers and not to mention the pastor of our church. This turned out to be a big undercover organization.

This business is as big as I originally thought. This is pretty heavy stuff. Toni said a girl the both of us knew was sleeping with her father. Her name is Carol she also sleeps with Kevin and John.

I started to think that the Williams were rich, if they had been doing the business for years and get paid many thousands of dollars for each baby. I started to think that if they gets paid as much as thousands of dollars a baby, that I need to be getting paid more than what they were paying me.

I wanted to wait until I could get Mr. Williams alone so I could talk to him in private about what he was paying me. I wanted him to find some time for us to talk. It has been very hard to be alone with Mr. Williams since I became pregnant.

I didn't anticipate falling in love with Mr. Williams. I was young, I didn't have a clue how to play this grown up game. It was too late this time. The next time I would be ready for anything.

Chapter 13

It's been two months since Sherry had her last baby. Now Suzanne was in the basement giving birth to her fifth child. It wouldn't be long before Mr. Williams would be jumping up and down on her again. There was a rage of fire burning in me knowing that Willie would be sleeping with Suzanne.

I had to find a way of coping with this jealousy brewing in me. Suzanne has had a baby boy. Mrs. Williams came upstairs to let everyone know.

I was thinking how soon it would be before they were back in the hay again. I knew by now he was sleeping with Sherry.

The rage in me was beginning to get the best of me when I thought of all the people he was going to be sleeping with including his fancy wife. Let's not forget the little school house females. I wished I could find some potion that would only make him rise when he was near me. That would burst his bubble. I had become so jealous of Mr. and Mrs. Williams' sleeping together. They should have been tired of each other, after all those years together. Well I hope that if I ever get to marry someday that I have a, till death do us part marriage while still making love.

When I would get home all I could think about was what female he was doing today. It has been three weeks since Suzanne had her baby and Sherry had hers two months before Suzanne had her child. I knew Willie had to be sleeping with both of them now. I was fighting mad.

I wish I could think of something to keep them apart besides killing them. I know that sounded extreme but I was weighing out all my options. I didn't want to be a killer but Mr. Williams was making me crazy.

I was not in a sound state of mind. All I knew was I didn't want any other woman touching him, not even his wife or daughters for that matter.

I was now three and half months pregnant. All I was thinking about was when I have this baby I won't have to hide sleeping with Willie anymore. I still had a long way to go. I was tire of trying to find a way to be alone with Willie. Sometimes I wondered if Willie even wanted to be with me anymore. He never makes the effort to be alone with me. I am beginning to doubt his love for me.

The Williams' had a visit from one of the ladies that went to the same church we went to. She turned out to be one of the many customers that they had. She was coming over to pick up Sherry's baby. Toni said they usually had a buyer right away.

The lady from the church had an emergency out of town, so she is just getting over to pick up the baby. Toni said her parents got paid twenty five thousand dollars for Sherry's baby.

I was blown away at the amount they were making from selling babies. I was imagining how much money they were worth. Toni said the bigger the business gets the greater the risk gets. I was not too focused on all that.

No matter what I am talking about my mind quickly turned back to Mr. Williams.

I told Toni it was beginning to be very dangerous. Toni said she guess her parents didn't care as long as her parents had the police and everybody that was of any important in their pocket they thought they would be protected.

Another month had gone by. Mr. Williams seemed like he didn't want to be bothered with me. I had to find a way to be alone with him. Everyone was out in the back yard. They were having a barbecue.

I saw Mr. Williams when he went into the house. I waited about ten minutes and then I went in the house. I finally had a moment alone with him. I asked him why he wasn't talking to me much. He said because he was not able to because his wife was always around. Then he said I needed to go back outside before his wife thought something was going on with us. I said wait a minute, he said what did I want from him? He then said us being together was just business and how many times did he need to tell me that? I said what about us? He said again, there is no us. I was fighting mad I wanted to scream. I was so hurt I went to Toni's room for a while. I was just lying there looking out the window watching Willie talk to every female that was out there. At least it seemed that way. The more I looked at him the more I felt like getting even. He can't dump me for his daughters and wife. All I was beginning to see was red. I wanted to kill someone. Maybe I would kill Willie his daughters or even his wife. My mind was going in a hundred different directions. I know deep down that I just was not going to kill anyone. I was just angry.

I had to find a way to calm down. I needed to think clearly. I had to really talk to myself. I felt so used. I thought about when we were together after I first got pregnant. He said he wanted to be with me. What a fool I was.

It was getting late and it was time for everyone to come in the house because the mosquitoes were out, bad. When Toni came inside her room she asked me what was wrong. I couldn't tell her because it was her daddy that I was mad at. I told her there was nothing wrong.

Toni didn't know she was the one that just saved me. When she came in the room, I had to get it together quickly.

I told Toni I wanted to go home. She asked me why? I said I just wanted to go home now. She said it was too late, that her parents might not take me home tonight. Toni said I will have to wait until tomorrow. I said ok.

I was wishing I was not pregnant but I was. So I had to find a way to make this pregnancy work for me. I thought if I go home for a while I could think with a clear mind after I got over being so upset.

I went to bed. It was hard for me to sleep. I was so upset. I might have felt a little better if I was able to at least slap Mr. Williams or one of his female dogs.

Morning came; I was not feeling any better. Mrs. Williams was cooking breakfast. I asked her if she would take me home. She said she had an appointment that Mr. Williams would have to take me home. Before I could think, I blurted out, "I don't want him to take me any place"

I thought about how that must have sounded. A second after I said that Mrs. Williams asked me why I didn't want Willie to take me home? I said I don't know I just wanted someone to take me. I didn't know what else to say. Then I said I don't care who takes me home as long as I get there. I was feeling like a fool.

I didn't anticipate any of this stuff that was going on with me. I was in a killing state of mind that I didn't like. I wanted to go at that moment before I said something that I would regret later.

Mrs. Williams said for me to eat some breakfast before I went home. I didn't want any but I ate anyway. After I was done eating Mr. Williams was going to take me home. I said ok. I said to Mr. Williams when are we going? He said he was ready. I jumped from my chair like it was on fire. I told Toni I would call her later.

Mr. Williams and I got in the car. We pulled out the driveway. I finally got a chance to give him a look I knew he didn't want to see. I was as quiet as a mouse.

Mr. Williams didn't know what to say. If he knew what was on my mind he would not have been able to drive the car. He finally broke the ice and asked me how was I feeling? What nerve did he have? I managed to get out "I am ok." He went on to say he was sorry. Then he said I caught him off guard, when I came in the house behind him. He said he didn't mean any of that he said. He said his wife was watching him closely. I asked him what reason she would have for watching him. He said his wife is ok when it's business otherwise she gets jealous. I didn't know how to react to that. I said, so you do care for me? He said he likes me a lot and he even thought he loved me. He then said he stands to lose a lot of what he has invested in the family business. Before I knew it I blurted out "I love you to". All of a sudden all the things I said went out of my head. I melted like ice-cream on a hundred degree day. Mr. Williams said no, for me not to say that I love him. He said I just think I was in love with him. I said ok.

Mr. Williams said maybe we shouldn't see each other for a while so you can think about things. Then you will find out you are not in love with me. Before I got out the car I asked him to say that he loved me. He looked at me like I was a damn fool. That was a dead giveaway. He told me he had to go, and he would see me later. I thought to myself I was glad he took me home because now I knew he was just lying about everything. I then knew I had to plan a surprise attack. They say revenge is sweet, I was about to find out. He was playing me like a deck of cards, because I was a little girl. He just didn't know I wasn't quite as naive as he thought.

Two weeks has passed since I was last at the Williams' house. Toni called me but Mr. Williams didn't make any effort to say hi to me. He was my father's friend he could have asked how was I doing but he didn't. That was the icing on the cake. I knew he didn't care for me at all. He only cared about selling my baby.

I wondered what he would have to say if I decided to keep my baby that he is the father of. Wow that's a thought. I really didn't know what I was going to do but I knew it was not going to be nothing nice.

I was beginning to think long and hard about what revenge I was going to take out on Mr. Williams.

I needed a getting even handbook. I wanted to get even and then some. I knew I had to get over being so mad. I had to make him think I was ok with everything. I wanted to get him good, but I didn't want to hurt myself in the process of getting even with him, because what goes around comes around. That statement made me think was I ready for my pay back. I can't worry about that now. I just wanted him to pay.

Chapter 14

Another three weeks had gone by and I still had not been over to Toni's house. I called to talk to her. She said she was tired of being pregnant all the time. I could tell over the phone that Toni was very unhappy; she has not had a chance to be a kid. I asked her what she was going to do about all of this getting pregnant stuff. She said she didn't have a clue.

Toni and me was just teenagers, the both of us had just turned fifteen, but living life as adults. Becoming parents to children we would never get to see after birth. I was beginning to think I wasn't going to be ok with someone else raising my baby, especially in the same town.

The weekend was here. I thought it was about time for me to go back over the Williams' house if I wanted to get even with Mr. Williams.

We were talking about going to the store tomorrow. I told Toni to ask her parents if I could come over. So she did. They said yes, so Mrs. Williams came over to get me.

When I got over to the Williams' house I looked at Mr. Williams, the way he made love to me came to mind. I had to shake it off.

Toni asked me if I were going to the store with them after breakfast. I said I didn't have any money. I was waiting for one of the

Williams to say they would take care of it like they used to. I waited and waited. To no avail they didn't say anything. I was very upset. Before I agreed to go into the family business they were kissing my butt. They just didn't know they were making my revenge sweeter.

Everyone was getting ready to eat breakfast. Mrs. Williams cooked some bacon and sausages. I sat down to the table. I was trying to do everything I could do not to have an attitude with Mr. and Mrs. Williams. It was hard, but I managed to get past it.

After everyone was done eating all the girls got into the car to go to the store. I was left alone with Kevin and Mr. Williams. Kevin was still in bed in the basement. So that meant Mr. Williams and I were almost alone. I must say I was still feeling him. I wanted to throw my arms around him and say I was sorry. I don't know what I was sorry for, but it didn't seem to matter at that moment. I wanted him to throw me down to the floor and make stupid no holds barred love to me. Being alone with him was making me get very emotionally weak. The love I felt for Mr. Williams was trying to overpower my revenge. I did let it get the best of me. He was looking mighty good to me. I was hoping he would try something.

After about ten minutes he started to talk to me. He asked me how I was doing with the pregnancy. I said just fine. Then he came out with a question I was not expecting, well I guess I was not expecting any type of conversation. But this question almost made me turn a flip. He asked me was I still in love with him? I swallowed hard and said yes. I didn't know if I should have said that or not but I did. I saw him smiling at me. I asked him what was wrong. He said he was hoping I was because he was still in love with me. You can imagine how happy I was; especially when he grabbed me and said he couldn't wait any longer to touch me. Then he was kissing me hard and passionately at the same time. It felt like I was dreaming, I tried to stop him even knowing I didn't want him to stop. I was afraid he was going to hurt me again. I didn't want to focus on that because he was making me feel so good. I was just too weak for him. I couldn't hold out any longer. I kissed him so hard

I thought I was going to swallow his tongue. It was so good, words couldn't justify the way I was feeling.

He could get me to do anything he wanted. He could have told me to crawl. I just may have if he was crawling behind me. So I was weak and being a baby myself I couldn't compete with a strong adult male. He held me so tight; it almost felt like he really did love me. Was I being naive? Most likely, at that moment I really didn't care much. He was not only making love to my body he was making love to my mind. The way Willie made me feel I would have thought that he loved me. Let's face it I was a little small town girl in a big man's world. I was not ready for grown up games. As long as Mr. Williams was making love to me the way he was I was willing to spread like an eagle whenever and wherever. He made love to me for hours. We had to end our love making if we didn't want to get caught. After we were done taking a shower Mr. Williams got in his car and left. I didn't care where he went at that time. He left me feeling good. I was totally satisfied.

The time was rushing by, it was one o'clock, and the girls were back at home. Mrs. Williams asked me where her husband was. I told her I didn't know. If she only knew her husband had just shaking me up like a salt shaker, and it was not even business. I was so happy. I was giving everyone a hug. I even gave Mrs. Williams a hug. She just didn't have a clue. I know that sounds bad but I couldn't help myself. I needed to calm down. I knew what I was doing was wrong; maybe that's why I had been having so much bad luck. You know that when you set a trap for someone you better set two. After a few days I calmed down, I had to snap back into reality.

They were back to business as usual. I found out that Mr. and Mrs. Williams kept a log book locked up tight. I had to find a way to unlock the file cabinet. In the mean time I had to just keep a log of my own on all the activity I saw and heard around the house.

I needed to get a camera so I could take a picture of the delivery room in the basement. I started writing down when people came over to the house. I wrote down phone calls they were making and receiving. I wrote the times and dates on everything.

This time I was going to have a hold card. A girl shouldn't be caught without one. I was spending a lot of time trying to find evidence on the Williams'. I was hoping I would never have to use it. I had to think of a good plan in case I would need it at a later date.

I had to think of a way I could have a camera in the house that wouldn't look suspicious. It would have been nice if I could get a picture of one of the deliveries. I knew that was a little farfetched at this day and time. There was not all this modernistic technology around back then like now.

My pregnancy was coming along slowly. It was beginning to get harder and harder to carry the baby. I was already thinking about not doing this anymore.

Thursday morning was here and breakfast smelled good. I got myself all cleaned up and went downstairs and sat at the kitchen table to eat, when all of a sudden I became nauseous. I had to rush to the bathroom. I was in there for a while. I was not able to eat anything. I went back upstairs and started to read a book I had gotten from the library a few weeks back.

I needed to have this baby. I still had a few months to go. I was thinking of a way to lose this baby. I was very confused because I know I was selling the baby but I wanted a part of Mr. Williams at the same time. I was getting very tired of being pregnant

I was lying down when I heard Mr. Williams calling me. I got up and went down the stairs to see what he wanted. When I made it down the stairs I saw Mr. Williams lying on the sofa with nothing but a robe on. He asked me to sit down beside him. I asked him where everybody was. He said they went to the grocery store. I must have been looking very strange, because he asked me what was wrong. I said I didn't know yet. I said I was a little sick to my stomach. Mr. Williams asked how long I have been sick. I said it started yesterday. He said the flu was going around. I wanted to say pregnancy was going on around here, but I didn't. Then he said I may be ok in a few days. I said I hope so.

Mr. Williams started to rub my stomach and kiss me on my hand. For some reason I didn't want him touching me, being next to him made me sicker. I guess it must be because I was pregnant. He could tell I didn't want to be bothered.

The more I pulled away from him the more he tried. I said Willie I am not feeling good. I told him I needed to go upstairs and get back to bed. He said to me "why you don't want to be with me?" I said I was sick. I need to lie down. He said I will lay down with you.

He said his wife wouldn't be back for a few hours. I just didn't want him to touch me.

When Mr. Williams lay down next to me I just wanted to kick him out the bed. It popped in my head if I wanted to get some evidence I needed, I had to be cool. So I let him make love to me. After awhile it started to feel good to me.

After about twenty minutes he got up and went back down stairs. A few minutes ago he had hours to be with me, isn't that peculiar. As usual all he wanted from me was sex, like always. After I got cleaned up I went back down stairs and into the living room where he was sitting. I sat down next to him, when I tried to hold his hand he pulled away from me, and said I should go back upstairs before his wife came back. The fool acted like I didn't remember him saying his wife was going to be gone for hours. I'll just let it ride. I became so upset I forgot I was sick. I had to be cool to accomplish what I wanted to do, so I just pretended I was ok with it.

A few minutes later Mrs. Williams was back. That was a well planned out strategy. He knew all the time they were coming back soon that's why he was rushing to get me in bed, that dirty dog. I had to keep reminding myself of what I was trying to do. The only thing he did was make me more determined to get him.

Today was Friday and the weather was sunny and bright. I was happy at the moment, but that changed in a few seconds. It was about twelve pm. Mr. Hatcher the principal was parking his car in the yard. When Mr. and Mrs. Williams went outside to greet Mr. Hatcher I got a camera and went upstairs to the window in Toni's room.

I had to plan very carefully not to get caught taking pictures of them. I had the curtain pulled back just enough for the camera. I was able to take a few pictures without them knowing. Mr. Hatcher stayed longer this time. I was able to get even more pictures.

I managed to get a picture of Mr. Williams giving Mr. Hatcher a yellow envelope. I wrote down the time Mr. Hatcher came over and when he left. An hour later a teacher from my school came over. She stayed outside. Mr. and Mrs. Williams told us to stay out of sight; he didn't want anybody else knowing what they were there for.

I got a chance to take a picture of Mrs. James, that's the teacher's name. After a few minutes a girl got out of the car. She looked to be about sixteen. You could clearly see she was pregnant. She seemed to be in a lot of pain. She looked like she was about to burst at any minute.

I took pictures of her, too. Mrs. Williams came in the house and told us to stay upstairs because she was going to have company in the basement. Toni looked out the window to see the girl. She refreshed my memory that that was a girl from school named Lisa. Lisa stopped coming to school for a few months before school was out for the summer.

As they were coming in the house I was not able to take pictures, they would easily see the flash. I wrote down details of what I seen and heard. As they were down stairs I heard Lisa screaming.

I guess she was having her baby. All of a sudden I became terrified about having this baby because it had to hurt the way Lisa was screaming. When I got away from Toni I would stand by the basement stairs to listen.

After about five minutes I heard Mrs. Jane the nurse say something was wrong. She said the baby was coming out feet first. As I was writing I heard silence. I didn't know what was happening.

I wished so bad I could see everything. Soon after Mrs. James was crying frantically, she kept saying my baby's dead, my baby's dead. My heart almost dropped to the floor. I became very nervous. I didn't know what to do. I had to hurry back up the stairs.

All of a sudden a cold chill came over my body. Mrs. Williams called and asked my parents could Toni and Sherri come over with me while she took care of some business? My parents said of course.

Mr. Williams took us to my house. I didn't know what was going on. It felt like I was dreaming. A few hours later Mrs. Williams called our house and asked to speak to my mother. She asked could the girls spend the night.

I was about to drive myself crazy wondering what was going on at the house. I could hardly sleep. All I was thinking about was if Lisa was dead. I asked Toni was Lisa ok? She said Lisa was alright. I ask Toni why we had to come to my house. Toni said sometimes when a girl is having a baby they don't want us there.

I was thinking if I just had a picture of Lisa having the baby. Back then we had never heard of a personal video camera. They had cameras or telephone. We had never heard of a portable telephone. Let along a camera being on one. It was now about two o'clock in the morning. I had to try and get some sleep. But I could not stop thinking about Lisa. I was so afraid for her.

It was now seven in the morning. I had falling asleep. I needed the rest. When I got up I started to think about Lisa again.

Mama was up cooking breakfast. She had cooked sausages, bacon, and even ham and eggs. Mama even made some of her homemade syrup and biscuits, and we drank milk and orange juice. I felt a little nauseous.

I managed to keep it down. I asked Toni to call her house to see what time they were going to pick us up. Toni called, there was no answer. With no one answering my imagination ran away with me. I just couldn't be at ease. I wish I could have been a fly on the wall. All I could do was just wait and wait. I had to find something to occupy my time. All of us girls went for a walk to the levee.

We were talking about the boys at our school, that subject kept us busy for a while. When we made it back home Mrs. Williams' car was in the yard. I was glad because I wanted to know what was going on. Mrs. Williams stayed at our house for hours. I was mad because I wanted to go back to the Williams' to see what was going on. Mrs. Williams was acting differently. She seemed nervous. Mama asked her what was wrong. She said nothing. I just didn't get much rest, she said. She did look a mess.

Mrs. Williams told us it was time to go to the house. We all got in the car and went on our way. It seems to be taking a long time to get there. Finally we were a block away. When we pulled in the yard I jumped out the car and went into the house. It was a feeling of calmness. It just seemed so different.

I decided to go in the basement, there was Mr. Williams, and he was holding a baby. I asked him whose baby it was. He said she belonged to one of his friends. He would not say a name. I needed to be looking out the window to see who picked her up? Mr. Williams asked me to hold the baby while he went out to the car. When he left I hurried up the stairs and got the camera to take a picture of the baby. When Mr. Williams came back inside he took the baby back.

I went outside in the back yard. I noticed some beautiful tulips. They were a beautiful yellow. They were in one corner of the yard. There was also some dirt that had been moved. Something told me to take a picture of that spot, so I did. I started having thoughts of someone being buried there. I wrote down how the tulips were not there yesterday. I had to be very careful that no one would catch me. I made sure no one knew what I was doing. Not even Toni. I was just gathering up evidence in case I needed it in the future.

I had another three months before I had my baby. Julia is now pregnant again; she says she's two months. Renee had four children.

She came over to the house to let everyone know that she's quitting the family business, because, She was getting married soon.

Mr. Williams lost it. He was angrier than I had ever seen him. He hated to lose the money he was making off Renee.

Renee asked everyone did they want to meet him, he was in the car? Mr. Williams said hell no. Everyone else wanted to see him.

Because Mr. Williams didn't want to see him, we all had to go to the car where he was.

I had never seen him before. After Renee's quitting, Mr. Williams asked her never to come to his house again. Mrs. Williams was upset with her husband. She tried to talk to him about it, but he didn't want to hear it. Renee had already sold four babies for them, what more did he want? Renee got into the car and drove off.

Mrs. Williams didn't talk to Mr. Williams for two days, she said she was going to let him cool off for a while. Mr. Williams was so mad he didn't want to talk to anyone.

A few days later the baby Lisa had was still there. Someone was supposed to pick her up today. I was listening and looking at every thing. I couldn't stay out the window because I was waiting to see who was picking up the baby.

Later that afternoon I saw a car pull in the back yard of the Williams house. Lord behold, it was the pastor and his wife. They came to pick up the baby. That freaked me out.

I was so upset because I couldn't get a picture of them because I ran out of film. The people coming over to get the babies would have been some good evidence. I wanted to kick my own butt. All I could do was to write it down.

Toni called me up the stairs. When I got up there, she had to tell me something. Then she said you will not believe how much money my parents got for that baby. I asked, how much? Toni looked at me and said thirty thousand dollars. I paused for a minute, and then I said for real? She said yes. I asked Toni did they have that money in the house. She said they had to have it here because the banks had already closed for the day.

I wanted to see all that money. I had never seen that much money before. I told Toni I wish I could get a good look at it. Toni said they locked it up in a safe in the closet. I told Toni I wish I could just get a good look at it. I asked Toni had she ever seen that much money before. She said yes.

She says her parents had been doing the business for many years. Toni continued by saying they had helped a lot of people who couldn't have kids. When Toni made that statement I knew she was still brain washed. I needed some way to get the log book. Renee stayed on my mind after her daddy just used her and didn't want anything to do with her after she was done having babies for him.

I loved Mr. Williams, but the way he did his daughter really upset me deeply. I started to think what kind of man I had fallen in love with. About two months had passed since the last time we had seen Renee at the house. Since she told everyone she was going to get married that was when she quit the family business to get married.

Renee had sent her family an invitation to the wedding. Mr. Williams said he was not going. He was still angry that she was getting married and not wanting to have any more babies for them. I couldn't believe he was still angry at Renee for wanting to live her life.

The date for the wedding has been set for the upcoming Saturday. Mr. and Mrs. Williams were fighting. Mr. Williams said he was not going to the wedding.

Saturday the day of the wedding came and Mrs. Williams didn't go to the wedding neither, so that meant we were not going. I didn't know these people were this cruel? They were beginning to scare me. I felt that I needed to get away from them soon.

I was watching the news on TV. I just could not believe what I was hearing. They had a picture of Lisa on the news. She had been missing for awhile.

They even said she was nine months pregnant and just had vanished without a trace. I knew I had to tell someone what was going on. But I was caught in a tight spot. I loved my friend Toni. I was thinking what would happen to her if I was to go to the police. "I need help".

Chapter 15

School had been in for a few months now. I was happy because It was getting very hard just hanging out. I had just too much time to spend on all this madness.

While Toni and I were in class I noticed she was moving around in her seat like something was hurting her. Toni had gone into labor. When Toni called home her mama came and picked us up.

Mr. and Mrs. Williams let me stay downstairs with Toni while she was in labor. I knew this may be the only chance to be able to take pictures of someone having a baby.

So I asked Toni could I take a picture of her in labor. She wanted to know why. I had wanted them for my scrapbook. Then I said when it's my time you can take pictures of me. It took some convincing but she finally said yes. So I took the pictures just before Mrs. Williams and Mrs. Jane came down the stairs.

Toni was in bad pain. After about three hours Toni had a beautiful baby girl. Toni started to have second thoughts about giving her baby up.

Mr. Williams took the baby away quickly. She was screaming for her mother to give her baby back. Of course she didn't. She was a very cute baby girl. I don't know if I could really do that even though it was for the money.

The same day Toni had the baby I saw a man from our church come and pick the baby up. They seemed to be selling most of the babies to the congregation at our church. I just didn't understand why they would do that.

I thought there would be a bigger risk with most of the clients being from our church. When I went to church it really freaked me out knowing a lot of the babies were being sold to members of our church. I couldn't believe our church was doing the unthinkable.

I wondered how I could sell my baby if it was going to be in the same church I was a member of. I didn't know what I was going to do. I knew all of this seemed to be wrong. I was still fifteen I didn't know what to do. I was having my baby in a few months. All I knew was I was not about to go crazy wondering if one of those babies were mine.

Toni said they had most of the customers from our church and at our school than anyplace else. I also knew that if I was to go through this I wanted more money than what they were paying me. Fifteen hundred dollars was nothing compared to what they were getting. Toni said Renee, and Sherry was getting paid a lot of money. Their parents were not giving her or Julia much money; they said they needed the money to take care of them. I asked what about Suzanne, she lives here to. Toni said Suzanne always had money. Don't forget she's daddy's favorite.

Then Toni asked me how much I was getting paid? I said fifteen hundred dollars. Toni proceeded to tell me that was not enough compared to what they get for selling each baby. Toni said she has seen her parents selling babies for fifth thousand dollars.

I knew that they were getting paid much more than ten thousand dollars for their babies, but I couldn't let them know I knew anything about what they were making.

Toni said she got a look at the log books and they were getting paid a lot more than ten thousand dollars for the babies. Toni said they just wanted us to believe they were only getting ten thousand dollars. I asked Toni how she got a look at the log book. She said she found out where the key to the file cabinet was.

I let Toni believe I didn't believe they were getting paid that much money. So Toni said the next time her parents went some place she would show it to me. That was just up my alley to get Toni to volunteer to let me see the books.

I just had to find a way to get a copy of it. I didn't have a clue how I was going to take pictures of it. I just needed for Toni to leave me alone with the books. I think the only way was to ask her to get me something. That way I could snap pictures quickly.

I wish there was a way to take pictures of everything in that room. The books were the most important evidence. It was good to know that the Williams had to be at church for a meeting. Toni and I would be at home by ourselves. The other girls were out with some of their friends. I had to be in a clear mental state of mind to be able to keep what she was saying in my mind. I couldn't let her see me write anything down about the business.

So Toni proceeded to take me in the basement. She first took me back to the delivery room. I was so nervous because Lisa popped in my head. I didn't know much about Lisa besides her going to the same school we went to.

I was still in disbelief about Lisa being dead and buried in the backyard. While we were in the delivery room I notice there was a bloody towel in the hamper. When Toni turned her head I quickly grabbed the towel and put it in my pants. That would be some good evidence if it was Lisa's blood.

Toni said she knows there is a way she will be able to get out of the family business. I asked Toni what she was planning to do. She said since she couldn't do anything to her parents the only thing left for her to do was to run away. Toni said otherwise she will have to keep having babies for her parents.

Toni couldn't wait until she would be old enough to move out of her parent's house. She said she will get her a real job that won't have anything to do with hurting children. Toni will change that statement later in her life.

Chapter 16

It was a nice sunny cold day with dew on the trees and grass. The sun was very bright; it looked like a beautiful summer day. I was ready for another summer break already.

I was also ready to begin snooping around the house again. I asked Toni if she knew where the keys were to the room where the files were.

Toni said yes she knew where they were but she had to wait until her family went somewhere before she could get the keys. Toni began to get suspicious about why I wanted the keys to the records room. I asked Toni did she want me to help her to find a way to stop her father and brothers from having sex with her without getting them in trouble. Toni quickly said yes, but she wanted to know how I was going to do that. I asked her to just trust me. She said ok. I told Toni we would find a way not to hurt her or her family. I knew it was a lie. But I had to reassure her. Toni's parents were getting ready to go out to visit some friends. They asked did we want to go with them. Toni said no, that she would stay there with me because I was not feeling very well. When they all left Toni went to her parent's room to get the key. She didn't want me to know where in the room the keys were hid, so I didn't go in there with her.

Toni gave me the keys to the records room. I asked Toni to stay at the basement stairs incase her parents had to double back for something that she could let me know. I had to hurry and take some pictures of everything I saw. I had to be careful that Toni didn't know I was taking any pictures of anything or else it would all be over.

When I was in the records room I almost fainted when Mr. Williams caught me. Toni had gone to the bathroom without letting me know. I was so afraid. I was happy I had put the camera back in my pocket. I did have the records books in my hand. I had to think of something fast. I asked myself how I was going to get out of this one. I made up a lie that I was wondering what was in this room. I played stupid. I asked Mr. Williams what was this book? I pretended to start to open it in front of him so he wouldn't think I had already seen it. I had seen it and took pictures of it to. Mr. Williams snatched the ledger out of my hand. Then he asked me how did I get in the room? I said the door was unlocked. I told him I was just bored so I was trying to find something to do. He said that the room was always locked. I said it was not locked this time. Mr. Williams said he was sure that room was locked, and then he said maybe his wife forgot to lock it and that he would ask her about it. Then he said I needed to leave the room so he could lock it. I thought I may have pulled it off, but I knew one thing I had to execute my plan quickly and get out of that house fast now. I was upset with Toni. She could have gotten me killed. This was serious business.

I told Toni that her father had come back for his wallet and caught me in the records room. Toni's face became flushed, and then she said she had to go to the bathroom. I told her she was no help. Toni asked me did her father know that she had given me the key. I told her no, I told her that I told her daddy that the door was already opened. Toni was so afraid that she told me to give her the key so she could put it back. I knew then that I had to finish everything I was going to do. I had to get out of that house as soon as possible. I thought I may have pulled it off, but I had to watch every step I made from then on. So they wouldn't have any thought that I was out to get them.

It was dinner time; we all set at the dinner table. This particular time Mr. Williams cooked dinner. I didn't think he knew how to cook. Mrs. Williams was always cooking, I never saw Mr. Williams even make a piece of toast. After dinner Mr. Williams took me home. I asked him when we were going to be able to be alone, because I missed him. He said he couldn't be with me anymore, and that maybe I should just stay away until it was time for me to have my baby. I was so hurt I could have killed him on the spot. He was treating me like I was a wet food stamp. I asked him if he still loved me. He said he never did. My heart felt like it had fallen to the floor and someone was stomping on it repeatedly.

I began to cry uncontrollably. Then he said he didn't care about me crying. He said it was time for me to get out of his car. If I had a gun I would have shot him dead over and over again. I told Willie I was not getting out. He said yes I was and now. To stop from having a confrontation in my parent's yard I got out of his car. I had become enraged with hate. I had to have some time to think about my next move.

It had been two weeks since Mr. Williams had put me out of his car. I had seen Toni at school. I asked her how her family was doing. She said they were doing just fine and at business as usual. I got upset just to know Mr. Williams was doing just fine. I wanted him to hurt just like I was hurting.

When I got home from school I told my parents that when I was over to the Williams' house I had slept with Mr. Williams and gotten pregnant. I told my parents that Mr. Williams had made me sleep with him and that it had been going on almost a year now. I also told them that the Williams' were going to sell my baby. To my surprise my parents were not shocked. Their reaction to what I had just told them was unbelievable. I just didn't understand. The only thing they said was maybe it would be best if I just stopped going over to their house. I was blown away. Then I asked my parents what was I going to do about being pregnant? My father just said I would have to give the baby to the Williams' so they could take care of everything since Mr. Williams was the one that did this.

For some reason I thought my father would go over to the Williams' and kick Mr. Williams tail at the least. I felt like my family may have known all about this business. I then thought to myself no, my parents would not have known anything about all this. They must have been in shock. Whatever they were going through I just didn't understand.

It was close to the time for me to have my baby. I was beginning to have pain every once in a while. I had never had a baby before so I didn't know how it would feel to go into labor. I was so tired and big that my back hurt all the time, but I was beginning to feel pain in the lower part of my back and stomach every fifteen to twenty minutes. I told my mama that I was hurting bad every so often that It felt like something was wrong. Mama said that it sounded like I was in labor. I asked her what I should do. She said for me to call Mr. Williams and tell him I was in labor. I really didn't want to, but I had to have this baby some place. My parents was not going to do anything because they said that Mr. Williams was the one that got me into this trouble so he will have to take care of it. When I called Mr. Williams and told him I was in labor he asked could my parents bring me over there. I told my mother what he said and she said she will take me over there. I asked her was she going to leave me over there by myself. She said yes and that she will come back when my labor pains was closer together. I was very afraid to be alone over there by myself. I didn't have much of a choice. So I went to the Williams. When we got there Mrs. Jane was already there. My pains were getting very bad. I wished my mother was with me. I was beginning to think that they were upset with me for sleeping with Mr. Williams without telling them sooner.

It was time for me to go to the delivery room. I was calling for my mama. I asked Toni to call my mama. She said she would. When she was going to call Mr. Williams told her not to call. I asked him why not? He said that everything would be ok. I said no I wanted my mama. They didn't pay me any attention. Toni said she had to do what her parents told her to do. I was crying and screaming at the same time because the pain was so bad. Toni did stay in the room with me. The nurse said that I still had a ways to go. I became terrified that I had to go through this pain for a long time. I asked Toni to please sneak and call my mama. Toni said she couldn't. I begged her to call. She said she would be in a lot of trouble. I wanted to die because the pain was so bad. If I had a gun next to me I would have shot myself or Mr. Williams for doing this to me.

On top of all this pain I became so afraid for my life because they didn't want my parents to come over. I didn't have any protection. They can do anything to me. I asked Toni not to leave me and could she stay with me when I have the baby? She said if her parents let her. If they don't let Toni stay with me I would become so afraid of what they might do to me.

I was wondering why my parents didn't just come over to check on me. I just couldn't understand why my parents were doing that to me. After about five minutes my mama came in the basement. I was hurting so bad but I managed to put a quick smile on my face when I saw her. I wasn't as afraid of them doing anything to me when my mama was there.

This big pressure was in my lower stomach made me bare down and I began to push without trying. The baby was coming and it was coming quick. Mrs. Jane rushed to the basement just in time. She told me to push every time I have a pain. It took only three pushes and the baby was there. I was so glad that was over. I wanted to see my baby but they wouldn't let me. I asked my mama can I see my baby. She said it would be for the best if I didn't see the baby. I told my mama I wanted my baby, that I had changed my mind about giving it up. Mama said it was too late that the baby was gone. I said no mama please get my baby. She just said I was too young to raise a baby, and to just hush. I cried and cried. They didn't even let me know if it was a girl or a boy.

After I was all cleaned up I was so tired that I could barely speak but I was not about to stay over the Williams' house. I was so upset that I was angry with everyone. I didn't want to talk to anyone not even Toni for about two weeks. I was also mad at my mama but I loved her so, that I forgave her. Maybe I was too young to raise a baby being just fifteen, but I was not about to let the Williams get away with anything. The time had come for me to get back at them.

I decided to execute my original plan to turn the evidence I had over to the proper authorities. I had to be very careful because the Williams' were in a situation that they had a lot to lose. All that popped in my mind was that the Williams' had a lot to lose so I was afraid I might have come up missing. I became very nervous. The Williams could be plotting how to get rid of me if they became suspicious about me. I had to work extra fast so they wouldn't find out it was me that was going to turn them in. I was afraid that I might get caught. But I was determined to go through with my plan. This was not a game anymore. It had become sort of a challenge to play an adult game, but now it was a matter life or death. I was terrified. I had to be careful if I wanted to survive this dangerous game.

Because I had to end this dangerous game I had to make sure I got rid of the Williams' so I could be safe if they suspected me. I began by mailing all my evidence to the local police department. The Williams had the local police department in their pocket but I decided to send them a copy of the evidence anyway to shake them up. I sent one to the school board, the chief of police and the state police department. I had in the evidence all the names of the people that had done business with the Williams'. I had the bloody towel and I told them about the flower bed in the back yard. I gave them everything I had.

Chapter 17

After a few weeks I heard the authorities had started to arrest all the people associated with the baby selling ring. The police arrested The Williams' and the principal of my school. They picked up the pastor and his wife of my church. They arrested all the people that names were on the log book. The police were trying to find the underage girls that were having babies and selling them.

I was at home feeling good about Mr. Williams' being arrested, when I heard a knock on the front door. I asked who it was. I didn't hear a response so I opened the door. To my surprise it was four policemen. My heart felt like it was going to pound right out of my chest. I thought they were going to ask me about the Williams'. I asked what I could do for them. One of the officers said they were looking for Mr. Edward and Mrs. Weesie Jones. I didn't have a clue why they were looking for my parents. I called for mama and daddy to come to the door. When they got to the door the officers asked were they Mr. Edward Jones and Mrs. Weesie Jones, they said yes they were. One of the officers had a paper in his hand; he said to my parents that the both of them were under arrest for illegally buying and selling babies. Then they said you have the right to remain silent or anything you do or say would be used against you in a court of law. Then they asked my parents did they understand these rights?

My parents said yes. When they took my parents to jail, I didn't understand what was going on at all. I was very confused. All we could do was to wait for our parents to call home.

It had been three hours since the police took our parents to jail. When they called us my oldest sister was talking to them about the charges, the police said they had against them. Robin asked our parents what they wanted her to do. They wanted Robin to make an appointment to see them. They only asked Robin to come. I guess they asked her because she was the oldest at home and the rest of us had to go to school. The appointment they gave Robin was a week away. I didn't know what to do with a whole six days of waiting. My mind was going through all kinds of torment. I was trying to stop myself from going crazy. I didn't understand what was going on. I thought the police just had to straighten out some things. I decided to try not to worry much. All of a sudden it popped in my mind did my parents buy any of us and that my parents knew about the Williams' business from the beginning. My mind was working overtime. I was about to go crazy.

Thursday morning was here. Robin woke us up so we could get ready for school. It was very hard for me to concentrate on any school work, knowing that Robin had to go and see our parents to find out what was going on.

School was out. It seemed like the bus driver was driving extra slow. It could have seemed like that because I was ready to get home to see what was going on. When we made it there Robin had already went to see mama and daddy. When we got home Robin said she needed to talk to us about something that was very important. She asked us would we all meet her in the living-room in an hour. I was so afraid of what I was going to hear. I was so afraid that I was shaking very badly. I didn't even want to be there for the meeting, I was too nervous to eat. The time was just taking its own little sweet time.

The time had come for Robin and the rest of us kids to have a meeting. Robin said what she had to talk to us about was very important and that it would hurt us a lot but everything would be ok. My heart felt like it had dropped to the floor, and then Robin asked us were we ready? We all looked at each other and said "Yes". Robin started saying mama and daddy told her to tell us that they love us all and hope that we would continue to love them when we heard what they had to tell us. Robin said mama and daddy said no matter what they loved us all equally. I was anxiously anticipating what was going to be said next. Robin said to us that some of us were not their biological children. We all just looked at each other. I was in shock, but I knew what they could possibly be talking about. I just didn't know what to say. Robin said Amanda, Donavin, Daniel, Evelyn, Edgar, Marcus, Cliff and I were not their biological children, but all the rest of us belonged to them. Robin was not theirs but she knew it all the time. Most of the older kids already knew. I was in all this mess but at that time I didn't know who I was. It was a hard thing to swallow. I just couldn't believe my ears. I needed help so badly. I just wanted to die. I couldn't handle this on my own. What was I going to do? I had no place to turn to. What shall I do? Who shall I call on for help? Whoever it was I needed them now, and in a big way. I was about to lose it. Little did I know that on the ledger I gave to the authorities had my parents name on it also. I didn't take the time out to read the whole thing. I tried to set someone up, now I set up my whole family in the process. If this would not have come out I might have never known that my mama and daddy were not my mama and daddy. I had a lot of mixed feelings. I didn't know whether to hate the parents I have now or to hate the ones that sold me. I did know that I had to keep what I had done to my family a secret forever.

After a few days it started to really just sink in how much trouble I had gotten my parents into. This was their lives I destroyed; I kept track of all the court dates. The attorney for my parents said the evidence was overwhelming. He said with as much evidence that was against my parents the case was pretty much open and closed. The attorney said my parents had bought so many children that they were looking at life. I am going to be responsible for sending my parents to prison!

I was only fifteen years old. What would I do if they really went to prison? I began to think about my sisters and brothers not really being my sisters and brothers.

A month later it was time for my parents' trial. They plead guilty. I didn't know why they did it. Somebody said they knew they were going to prison. But since they plead guilty they wouldn't have to air out all of our dirty laundry, and by pleading guilty it would make their sentence a little lighter. So that was why they did it.

The judge asked mama to stand first. The judge proceeded by saying to mama you have torn many families apart. In doing so, you have changed their family roots. The Judge told my mother, I am ashamed of all the children that you have bought that may never know who their relatives were. Then he said to her, therefore you are to spend twenty to thirty years in the Women's Correctional Facility in West Wayne, Arkansas. When the judge said that, I felt as low as a rug. I really hated myself at that moment.

The judge then asked for my father to stand. The judge told my father that he was disgusted at all the lives he had participated in ruining and that he was amazed at how easy it was for him to destroy so many lives so he is sentencing him 25 to 35 years in the men's correctional facility in Pinewoods, Arkansas. Then the judge said case is closed then he left the room.

I just couldn't believe what I had done to my parents. With them now gone what was I going to do? Toni was suspicious about me being the one who set up our parents. I had to do a lot of convincing for Toni to believe I was not the one who did it, all that lost I didn't want to lose her too. I told her that I would have never turned in my own parents. After telling her that I think she believed me. She is never to know that I didn't finish reading all the names on the ledger and it is to stay that way forever.

In the end Toni and her sisters, who were not her sisters by blood because her parents had bought them from some other couple who had the same type of business. The girls found out they were not sleeping with their father and brothers.

I had ruined so many lives. Because of what I had done, Toni and the other kids didn't have any parents either. I destroyed policemen, teachers and a principal. Not to mention all the kids they sold and bought. I hope no one ever found out I was the one responsible for destroying all of those lives even my own. The Williams not only had all of those cases for selling babies, but then there were the dead babies buried in the back yard along with that little girl Lisa. The sentence for the Williams' was life without parole for the murder charge.

Chapter 18

I was to blame. I wanted to kill myself. I didn't think about all the other lives that would be going down with the Williams'. I decided to just run away because I wasn't going to let them put me into foster care. Toni decided to go with me. We just needed to figure out where we were going to go. I didn't want to leave my little sister, but I knew that I couldn't take her with me because I couldn't drag her around not knowing where I was going myself. The best thing for me to do was to let her go to foster care so she could have a place to stay and eat. I had to leave her.

Since I had destroyed everyone including the church in my process of revenge I was feeling pretty bad. I destroyed the pastor and his wife who also went to prison. There was a whole list of names. I didn't even bother to read the entire log book. Most of the congregation from my church was in jail. They had to start their whole church all over again. I needed to leave town quickly before anyone figured out that I was the one who helped send all of those people to prison.

I needed to talk to Toni about where we were going to go. We were to meet in the park at midnight. When I arrived Toni was already there. We didn't know where we were going, so we just walked around for hours, and finally we decided that we would go to Michigan. I wanted to get as far away from Arkansas as I could.

We had a little money, but we couldn't use it for the bus. Once they found out we were gone they would check the bus and train stations. Toni and I decided to hitch hike a ride to Indiana. Since we hitchhiked so far we figured it was safe to catch a bus to Michigan. We decided we would go to Canton, MI. We didn't know much about it, just that a friend of mine had moved there a couple of years ago, her name is Angel.

We had finally arrived in Canton, now we needed to figure out where we were going to stay. I didn't know where my friend Angel lived or how to go about finding her. So we pretended we were older and stayed in a shelter. After we rested I looked in the phonebook to see if I could find Angel's address and phone number. I got lucky; Angel's phone number was listed. Angel was a few years older than I was and had her own house. Toni and I were lucky that Angel let us stay with her. After a while Toni fell in love with some older man and after dating him for a while they got married.

Since Angel and I had been hanging together for a while now, Toni's move made me and Angel much closer. Angel had become closer to me than Toni and I was. I could talk to her about almost anything. I wish I could talk to her about all the people's lives I have ruined, but I guess I just couldn't. I was afraid I would lose her as a friend. I couldn't take that chance, even if Angel always understands she might not be able to deal with this situation. She is always there when I needed her. I am blessed to have her in my life. Angel is the most beautiful, sweet, loyal friend anyone could ever have. I couldn't risk losing her alone with losing everything in my life already.

I remember a long time ago I laid eyes on one of Angel's Uncle's when I first met her. He was the most perfect vision I had ever laid eyes on. To this day I am in love with that man. I guess the love will always stay with me because I never got the chance to even touch him out of all these years.

His name is Terry. I often wonder if anything would become of us if I had stop running every time I laid eyes on him. He seems to go for those skinny type women. Terry always thought of me as a little girl, I was told. Well I have grown and he still doesn't pay me any attention.

If I could have gotten past acting like a kid maybe something would have happened. I don't know anything but I love that man no matter who enters my life.

Chapter 19

It had been three years since I left Arkansas. I was now an adult and the authorities couldn't do anything to me for running away. Turning eighteen took a lot off my shoulders. I felt at peace for the first time in my life.

One day Angel and I were out doing the grocery shopping, I had met this man. He was tall and slender, just like I like my man to be. I thought I had met the man of my dreams. His name was James I had been through so much that I had to take it nice and slow. He used to hold nice conversations with me all night long. We used to stay on the phone until one of us fell asleep. James was just what I needed at the time, even he became a nightmare. Since I was not able to have my dream man I had to settle for something else.

After asking me for four years to marry him I finally said yes, I accepted his proposal. I guess I got tired of him asking me to marry him, I just said ok for him to leave me along. I wish I would never have accepted his proposal. But anyway I did. Seven years after marrying this man the nightmare began. We were mostly happy for the most part. He would have been a good husband if he was a real man. He was a follower not a leader. He didn't show me that part of him until we were already married. After marrying him I found out about all the cheating. I had a few encounters with some of his female dogs, even some of my own so called friends, but I just kept hanging in there, because of love.

When we got married I wore an antique gold dress. My husband wore a black tuxedo with an antique gold vest and a bow tie. His best man was dressed like him. The bridesmaids wore black or white dresses.

I was one of those women who did not like to be alone. I had many choices but I stayed with my husband and kept letting him run me in the ground.

The man I married put me through so much abuse that I'm still amazed that I came out of it alive and in my right mind. Today I don't give him much thought at all. I don't want to know if he even exists. When I seen all the other times he had cheated I should have started running backwards at full speed, but I didn't, and he bit me like the dog he is. He worked at a factory and started to have an affair with a co-worker that was before we got married. I know I should have called it quits then, but I didn't.

Our marriage started to fall apart when he got a job at a local nursing home. A few months after starting to work there he started to cheat. This female person didn't even deserve to be called a lady. She was also married with a lot of children. She was dropping them like a litter on the streets.

I had been hearing about this female but I tried to ignore it. He started to stay out all night long. I started noticing he was never hungry when he got home from work. I soon found out it was because she had been keeping him "fed."

Its females like her that makes marriages seem like they are nothing any more. People like her do not give married people any respect. As long as they got what they wanted. Those are the types of females that don't have any morals or self respect. They think that they took someone else's man. She didn't take anything from anybody that was no good anyway because if they were, they would not bring trash into their homes like that.

I started to pay more attention to my husband reactions around the house. He was never smart so it didn't take much for me to find him out. He would have females calling our home or his cell phone. I would answer his cell phone when he was sleeping; he kept numbers in his pockets.

One day I went to his job because he left home hours before he was supposed to be at work. I parked in the back of the job parking lot. After about fifteen minutes went by guess who I saw pulling up in the parking lot? Yes, husband and the tramp. They spotted me and tried to get away, but they didn't know how to get away.

He tried to hide in her van. I went over and made him get out. I politely told him to get out of the van. I gave her some advice she ignored it. I told her I knew about my husband being a dog, and because the town was so small I didn't want him in her van again. I told her if she wanted him to come over to her house she had to pay for him a taxi. She disobeyed that order so I had to tag her.

I started hearing, rumors that jezebel was pregnant, yes jezebel is the kindest name I could think of to fit her. She was telling my husband he was the father. She told her husband that he was the father of her baby and another man could be the baby's father. Of course since my husband, not having much intelligence he took it hook line and sinker. The Maury shows "He's not the father." And he wasn't the father.

There is always a willing female waiting to get your man if he's a weak little boy. It didn't take much convincing my husband, I could say the sky is blue, a woman could say its purple he would agree with the other woman.

When I found out about this female being pregnant, and my husband admitted to me that it was his baby. I decided to forgive him for that one, but no more was he going to see her. I said whatever she needed for the baby, he and I would get it together, but he was not to go over there anymore. That was ignored; he just kept going back over there.

There was this one girl that I thought was my friend for years. The man I married was going with her. This girl was always at my house, and she was sleeping with my husband. She was a backstabbing snake. Someone should have chopped her head off and watched the tail moving around a few minutes before dying.

Every time I think about him cheating on me I wonder why they were bothered with this man. He was not even a little attractive. He didn't have a nice body at all. Then it dawned on me I fell in love with him myself. I had to think about why I fell in love with this man. Then a light went on in my head, he was an expert at eating more than lunch at lunch time, and breakfast and dinner. If he could manage to eat his "dinner" it would be hard to let that go because you could swear he had a Master's Degree in the business. It would have been hard to let that go.

My husband always came home when he was with her at around seven in the morning. On this particular day I decided to go to her house. I got dressed and drove to the drive through window at McDonald's. I ordered some orange juice, hash brown, and a sausage with cheese biscuit. When I was finished with my order at McDonald's I drove to the street she lived on. I parked two blocks from her house. I waited, about twenty minutes. Later they got in her van and proceeded to drive in the direction of my house. I followed them to the street one block over from my house. I was behind them when he got out the van. By them not being too bright up stairs they didn't see me behind them. So he walked to the house. I blocked her in. I then got out the car. I went to her van. I said to her, "you know you are going to get your "butt" kicked?" She again not being very bright, she said yes. She would not have gotten a beat down; if she had just did what I asked. Which was let my husband find another way to her house and back home.

After the confrontation between her and I was over. I got back in my car and proceeded towards home. When I got home he was looking like a kid that got caught with his hand in the cookie jar. So I said to him, I guess its ok for me to have a man to kick it with, so I got the phone and pretended to call a man, when in fact I was calling my female friend. He thought it was a man on the phone; I turned my back on him while I was talking to my friend, him being as tall as a tree got a 2x4 piece of wood and hit me from behind in the temple of my head. Mind you my husband was 6'7, I was only five feet three inches tall, and that must have really intimidated him. The sad thing was he didn't face me like a man, he hit me from behind. His own family was so ashamed of him. He should have hid from himself with embarrassment. My friend on the phone called the police when she heard him hit me over the phone. He went to jail, his female bailed him out.

Ladies if you suspect something is going on with your man don't go looking for trouble because you will find it and you will be the one hurt in the end. These men, when they get caught they just go on about their business and you are going to be the only one hurting because they don't care, because no matter if they get caught most times they want stop but you will be left devastated and in pain. When they leave the house you will always think they are out cheating. Then you will be pacing the floor waiting for them to come home. Even if they are not cheating you will think so, because they will have put you in that state of mind.

When I called the jail to see if he was still there, they asked me what was my name, I told them. The woman on phone asked me did I know there was a warrant out for my arrest for assaulting the girl friend? I said no. It was about four o'clock in the afternoon. I was not about to turn myself in that late in the evening because I would have to wait until the next day to see the judge. I went and got some money and turned myself in the next morning. I told the clerk I was turning myself in because there was a warrant out for my arrest. The clerk told me to have a seat. Shortly after that an officer came and fingerprinted me. The officer said we had to go across the street to the jailhouse, he asked me did I have any weapons on me, I said no sir. He opened the door of the police car to let me in. It was only a few minutes after I got there the judge called my name.

He asked me how do I plead? I said not guilty. The judge gave me a three hundred dollars signature bond. I signed the papers and went home. A few days later a female came to my door with a personal protect order. I didn't open the door because my eye was pretty bad, I would have never believe, in a million years that my husband a man that vowed to love, cherish and take care of me would try to kill me. I was so ashamed I didn't want anyone on his job to see what my husband had done to me. People on his job were cheering them on like it was a good thing. I wished my eye was not so bad because I probably would have opened my door and snatched her in my house and beat them like a runaway slave for coming to my house bringing a personal protection order, they would have needed a PPO for themselves.

Can anyone tell me why is it when someone is cheating on their spouse there is always a cheering section for the cheater? At his job the women was acting like I was the villain. I know some of those women have a husband that had cheated on them, but those women were on the side of the people that were doing wrong. I know that when I knew one of my friends or relatives were doing wrong I didn't condone it or neither did I get in the middle of it because I knew they were wrong, but I didn't love them any less. That was something they had to work out, like I had to on a few different occasions, when I knew I was wrong. You know what goes around comes around. They will get theirs, we all do. These women at his job need to be put in their place. When their husband cheats on them, and he will, they shouldn't say a word because they think it's ok to sleep around with someone else's husband. After all that I was still standing, he gave it his best shot, I refuse to go down. He almost died when I told him that I slept with his female's husband. He said "God that man put his hands on my wife, and then he started to cry. I know you can imagine the look that came across my face. He could dish it, but couldn't take it.

Don't get me wrong it was on and popping doing my own thing some times. Don't think for one minute that I didn't do anything because it wouldn't be true. I might have been just smarter than he was at keeping my good times away from him. That may be why I am paying for the things I have done. I hope my ex-husband will stop all this nonsense and settle down and be a role model for his son that he finally had.

I know I may have done some things I should not have done. I am paying for it too. I wonder if my husband and his girl paid for what they did. They may already be paying now. I will say a prayer for the both of them. I am for real, and it will be a good one to.

With all the things my husband put me through I became very depressed. I am still fighting to get back to where I was before I married him. I had become so depressed I secluded myself. People just don't know what a person goes through when they are depressed.

I used to think it was something you just get over; I soon found out that depression was a real illness. Depression could leave a person debilitated. You feel like giving up on life. Nothing means a thing anymore, you feel worthless, and ashamed you even wish you could curl up and die. Life doesn't mean anything to you anymore. The thing that kept me going was God; otherwise I may have not made it. I would stay in bed for weeks at a time. I would not answer the telephone or the door. I felt ugly, dirty, used, and every sad feeling a person could have, I had it. I was giving up on life. I didn't care what happened to me.

After my husband tried to kill me, I decided to press charges against him. When I went to court I had to get on the stand to testify against him. His freak was there with her lies. My public defender said I had a choice. I could let him plead guilty and he would get six months probation and after the six months probation if he didn't get into anymore trouble his record would be clear. I decided that was not enough for a man to get for almost killing me. I decided to go on with the trial. My lawyer advised me that my case was open and shut. That was a lie. My husband almost killed me. After all the evidence the judge found him not guilty.

The judge said if my witness that was on the phone with me that called the police when my husband almost killed me that would have made the case different, because she was the witness to hearing him hit me. Tell me how many women have a witness to their husband beating them? I always hear about how women won't press charges against their abuser, but when I did the judge spit in my face. That was the end of that, pressing charges on your husband for attempted murder. I would not press charges on my abuser again so I can look foolish. They stress that point to press charges when you are being in a domestic situation then they let him go. I guess we need to start living in glass houses, so a witness can see you getting your ass beat. I don't have any faith in the justice system. I will handle my own justice, but I will make sure someone sees me somehow.

After all that I still had to get prepared for my husband's female to press charges on me. I was so depressed when my court day came along I wasn't in the right state of mind, so I pleaded no contest. I had to because I was not able to listen to the same judge say you are guilty, with my husband and his female being there. I wasn't mentally strong enough. I didn't get any jail time I was thankful for that. The bad thing about that was that I had a domestic abuse record. I am not able to do what I went to school for. I always wanted to do work in the medical field. When all this happened I was a Certified Nurse's Aide, being a Nurse's Aide was the most rewarding job I had ever had.

I faulted myself for putting myself in that situation for so long. My husband was not worth it, not even a little bit. I thank GOD that I am so over him that I don't care what is going on with him. If I saw him with a woman I couldn't care any less. I may even push him up and down on her myself. But I felt he had the power to tell his girl not to press charges and just leave it alone because they had already did a lot of wrong to me, but again being not any kind of a man he didn't do that. Then I am to blame, I knew that I allowed them to have a hold on me by giving them what they wanted, on top of them and depression I just didn't defend myself.

After everything I had been through I was blessed to still be standing. They didn't break me. Someday they will be broken. I am better now than I had ever been, about him that is, but I do have my moments out of all that the mental abuse was even worse. Being called all kinds of names and nobody else would want me and I was ugly and fat on a regular basics was a terrible thing to a woman's self esteem. I should have known better. I looked better than that girl and every time I went out the door some man was trying to talk to me. I almost feel sorry for them because what goes around comes around. I am living proof of that. I honestly do wish them well.

Chapter 20

Well writing this book reminds me that, that part of my life is still taking a toll on me. I have panic attacks when I think of what my husband did to me. My depression leaves me in a self built prison. All I do now is read and write because I hate to get out the house at times. I get out a little more than I use to but when I am finished with what I have to do I am back home not wanting to do anything, because of my depression.

I can't seem to break away from it. I seldom leave the house because of my low self esteem. People are always telling me you are pretty or I am beautiful, but I don't see that most times. There are sometimes when I feel like I am pretty, but that's not often.

So many bad things had happen to me. I had to take so many different medications that I would just say, today I am not taking any medicine. I get so tired of all that medication that sometimes I feel like giving up.

I have high blood pressure, high cholesterol, diabetes, hypo thyroidism, hypo para-thyroidism, That is called Graves disease, depression, post traumatic stress from when my ex husband hit me in the head with a two by four board from behind. I have fibro myalgia, anxiety and panic attacks, and depression for all those problems I have to take medication for. I take a total of twenty five pills each day, most of them for the rest of my life unless the Lord says different.

I know that I just might have to live with it. I think of it as a punishment for all the wrong I have done in my life time. I accept that, what else can I do?

When I started functioning I took a trip to Indiana where I had met the brother of one of my friends. He was a very nice man, a complete gentleman. He was a real man I was not used to. He would open doors for me, pull out chairs for me, he would even take off my shoes and rub my feet rather I asked him to or not. He had a lot of class. I was there for a week; he treated me like a queen. He would wash my back when I bathe. Dean would compliment me throughout the day. He made me feel like I was a beautiful delicate flower.

That week was very special to me. I will never forget that time in my life. I fell in love that week. He spoiled me in all kinds of ways. I believe if he had the moon he would have given it to me. I had not smiled or laughed so much in a long time. We made love all over the place. In all kinds of positions we could think of.

Dean was older than my ex-husband, but he could make love at any given time. If I was ready he was ready. There was no waiting period for him. Imagine a man being able to perform at any given time, well I found him. My ex-husband was a thirty second man on a good day. When it was time for me to go home I was very upset. I didn't want to leave him, so I didn't, he came with me. He stayed with his sister because I was still married. I remember when we used to make love almost every time we were together. We could not keep our hands off each other. We made love before I went to work. Dean would be waiting on the porch for me, when I got home to his sister's house, Dean would make love to me again. I was always willing to let him have his way with me. That was the best love I had ever had. Dean was the person who was there helping me to cope with things. My depression had gotten so bad.

When a person is diagnosed with clinical depression, no one can bring them out of it except with the help of God. I don't care how much a person is in your life and behind you one hundred percent they cannot bring you out of depression, they can help you to cope with it sometimes. To have a person there for you when you are in a state of a mental relapse is a God sent. Thank you Dean. I had to have extensive therapy treatment. I was almost at the end of my rope. I was over the man that I married. I would even forget he existed. With my depression the only time I was at peace was when I was sleeping.

I had relived my ex-husband trying to kill me over and over again while writing and proof reading this book. My depression had gotten so bad that I starting having anxiety and panic attacks often. Those panic attacks were terrifying. My chest would hurt; I have a feeling of going crazy. Panic attacks would make me feel like I could just walk in front of a speeding car just to get it over with. I would break out into a sweat. This is the worst feeling I have ever had in my life. In fact, it was so bad I would never ever wish that feeling on neither my ex-husband nor his female friend. I give my ex-husband credit for teaching me how to love a real man, thank you very much.

Chapter 21

.

To be at peace I had to leave Michigan for my salvation. I had to think long and hard about my life. So I decided to move to another state. Some say you cannot run away from your problems, which is true to a certain extent, but I would be dead or in prison. I packed up what I could and got on the bus and moved to Kansas, a place I never stepped foot in before. I left everything behind that I accumulated for many years. Some say that's brave, I think it's more like survival. I was expecting to move to a small town, boy was I wrong. It was a city with lots of violence. It was a far cry from where I came from. When I first moved to Wichita, Kansas there was a serial killer on the loose.

I had stayed in Wichita, Kansas for three years now and I didn't like it much. I was expecting a little country town, it was hardly little. I was shocked at how big Wichita was. I have always liked the country living. I thought I was moving to a country town. I watched a lot of westerns and those shows talk about Wichita, they sure have changed totally. There was nothing like country in Wichita. When I made it there I quickly started to miss my man, so I rented a car and drove back and got my baby. He was very happy to see me and I was very happy to see him. I stayed a few days. I got my man and we went home. It was very nice to be with him again that however didn't stop my depression. Dean did all he could to make me happy. It's nothing funny about it; you could slowly be killing yourself if you don't get help. A person doesn't have to give in to depression, just get some help.

My Dean used to wake me up to a good breakfast. He would do all the cooking. He just enjoyed it. I don't care what he was doing he would find time to cook. I remember when I would say I wanted catfish, Dean would get up and cook me breakfast, then go to work. After work he would go fishing and bring the fish home, clean them, cook them and bring them to me in bed.

If I was sick he would lay in bed with me holding me, rocking me and singing me to sleep. Dean had some bad faults to, but not anything I couldn't deal with. The main one was his jealousy. He didn't want any man looking at me. The few other little things are not worth mentioning. He was a blessing to me. When I had to be admitted to the hospital he was there every day. Dean was the best man I had ever known. He was so kind and always giving. I always think of his smiles. He could brighten a power failure.

I remember when I was in the hospital, Dean came to see me. He would brighten up the place. He had patients believing that he was a doctor. He would walk through the hallways shaking their hands. This particular day Dean went into the T.V. room. He saw an organ and started to sing a love song to me that he was making up as he went along. It was a beautiful song.

My Dean loved to dance. He could dance better than young people. He had lots of energy and a lot of talent. I remember the first time we danced. I will never forget it because we danced to the O' Jays' song, Stairway to Heaven. It was so beautiful. Dean was so romantic. He was always cheerful, filled with love and understanding. You would not believe how wonderful he was.

Dean was so loving and caring; he loved his mother so much. He would go and see her every chance he could. That was one of the many reasons why I loved him so.

I had started to have those panic attacks more frequently. He would hold me and talk to me through it all. He loved to be funny. By the time I finished laughing I would forget all about the panic attack. He would get my mind on something else. Sometimes even being with me that couldn't stop my depression. I was always going to the mental health hospital where I would be for weeks. I needed to get some help. I was beginning to think about suicide.

After a few years went by, I thought I couldn't be helped. I was taking medication after medication. I thought I had to live with it or die. I asked the doctor what was wrong with me. He said I had a chemical imbalance in the brain. I asked him what could be done about it. The doctor recommended (EST) Electro Shock Therapy. They put you to sleep and shock the part of the brain that is Chemically Imbalanced. I was not ready for that.

Each time I got out of the hospital I would feel better for a little while. But the depression would continue to haunt me. I was becoming more depressed; I was not able to perform everyday tasks. When you know someone is depressed please remember depression is a real illness. Some people think you are just lazy and don't want to do anything but stay in bed all day. I wish more people would get more education about depression. It could be a matter of life or death. As time went by I just tried to take it one day at a time. Dean and I tried to deal with my depression as best as we knew how. He was very patient with me. Everyone you know is affected by your depression. Dean, I know he was suffering too. He would always pickup my responsibility in taking care of everything when I was going through. It's very rare to find a man like my Dean. If you find a man like my Dean you better hold on to him. Dean was always doing something good for someone. Even though he knew 90 percent of the time they were using him, but that didn't matter to him he did it anyway. Dean was a man who could do mostly anything. He was a mechanic, a carpenter and a builder he could even build a house. He had lots of talents. I never needed to call a repair man for anything as long as Dean was there.

Dean decided to go home to see his mother. He stayed there for a few months, while he was gone I moved out of my house because the bills were too much for me. I moved in with a friend for a little while. I didn't have a phone so I could not call him, but he would call my friend to check on me. I didn't get a chance to talk to him much doing that time. When I was done moving I called his mother's house to check on him, his nephew answered the phone. I wanted to let him know I was coming to see him. When I called and his nephew answered the phone, I said to him, where is your uncle? Was he out fixing on something? His nephew paused for a few seconds then he proceeded to tell me he had some bad news. My heart skipped a beat. He Began by saying his uncle passed away two weeks ago of a heart attack. At that moment I became hysterical. I put the phone down. After about a minute I picked the phone back up again, then I said to him, I'm talking about your uncle Dean. He said yes ma'am. I could not cope, I kept saying No, No, No. I had to get off the phone. I felt like I wish I could have died at that moment. I ran in my friend Devonda's room and told her Dean was dead, she got out of her bed; she looked like she was in shock. A few minutes later the phone rang it was his mother. I had to find a way to compose myself because that was her son she lost. It was very hard. I had to get off the phone. I asked her could she hold on for a minute she said yes. I was in no shape to talk to her. I asked my friend if she could talk to his mother for me, so she did. When my friend first got on the phone she had to pause for a few seconds, then she said hello. She went back to her room so she could talk to his mother. I was in the living room sitting on the floor in a daze. Then I started to get hysterical again. I asked my friend Devonda to get me to the hospital because I couldn't do this alone I needed some help. So she rushed to put on her clothes. When we got to the hospital I was still hysterical. It was running through my mind that, that was Dean's mother I couldn't imagine, what she might be going through. I was not coping with this at all. I wanted to die. They gave me a sedative. I was not able to control myself; I had to wait a while before calling her back. I had to get myself strong enough to talk to her. When I did get a chance to talk to her it was a few weeks later. She said she tried to get in touch with me but she couldn't because I didn't have a phone. I moved and I was the only person she knew in Kansas. I had to try to keep myself together for his mother; after all she lost a son. It was one of the hardest things I've ever had to do; it was so hard trying not to break down. I just could not compose myself so I didn't talk but a few minutes. I could not deal with this at all. I stayed in the hospital for four weeks.

With Dean's dying and my depression I didn't think I was going to make it. The only thing kept me going was the Lord. Otherwise I would have been dead or at least out of my mind. I had gotten so bad that I was visioning Dean being in a dark cold grave not being able to breathe. It was so bad I could see him dancing like a young boy. Every time I vision his feet moving I would break down, the vision was so clear. I thought about his friend dropping him off to our home and he gets in the middle of the street and dance and sing. His friend would say man you can dance. His friend said he can even sing. That was the image that kept repeating in my mind over and over again. Every time I saw that image of him dancing I would break down. Dean was so full of energy, I was almost sure I was going to lose my mind. I was feeling guilty about not being able to say good bye to my special man that would always be in my mind. It was haunting me about not being able to go to his funeral. It may have been a blessing that I didn't see him just laying there with no life in him, I might have really lost my mind. I just wanted to lie down and die, I miss his jokes. He was full of fun and surprises. You would never know from one moment to the next what he was going to say or do. I had to go through extensive therapy, to stay sane. I just knew I was going to lose my mind. I had to do a lot of praying to stay in my right mind.

As long as God kept me in my right mind I would not forget this one time I had to go the hospital. It was on a Sunday, I was in room seventeen. The doctor that saw me asked me a question; I had to think long and hard about what to say. He asked me who I turn to when I need someone to help me through a problem. I said God. He then asked me the big question. He said if I died today where do I think my soul would go? I didn't know how to answer that question. I knew that I believed in God, I read my bible regularly. It occurred to me that my soul would not be going to heaven. I knew then I had to get right with God. I became so frightened. The doctor said to me he was a Christian and if he died today his soul would go to heaven. Then he asked me if we could pray together. I said yes. He put his hands upon my head and started to pray hard, there were nurses walking in and out the room, but he didn't care he just kept praying. When I went to the hospital I was having chest pains, when he finished praying he asked me how I felt, it took a long time for me to answer that question because the pain stopped. The anxiety had gotten better, I just felt like a new person. It took me a long time to answer because I didn't want him to think that I was lying, but I had to tell him I felt better, later the nurse came in the room and asked me did I need some pain medication? I told her no.

I was still suffering from major depression. There is a depression due to every day stresses. Like being worried about how are you going to pay your bills, or if you've passed an exam. That kind of anxiety and depression go away when you pay your bill and find out you passed the test. But this chemically imbalance depression is tough to get through, especially when you have taken so many different kinds of anti depressant medications and they didn't work. There were so many times I ended up in the hospital because the depression had gotten so bad that I started to think of suicide. I started going to the mental hospital on a regular basis, staying two to four weeks at a time. I thought there was nothing that could be done; I thought I just had to live with it. I had to be admitted to the hospital about every few months. I didn't want to live anymore. The doctors recommended me to try (EST) Electro Shock Therapy again. They had recommended this to me before. That time I said no. But this last time when they asked me I said yes. My Dean was gone so I didn't much care about things at this point. They said I would have to have six to ten treatments. For two weeks on Mondays, Wednesdays and Fridays. They got me up at five a.m. and took me to another hospital where they did the treatments. When they did the first treatment I had a headache for a few hours. I didn't notice anything for a while. After about five treatments I was released from the mental health hospital. I forgot about the treatments, but after a few months it dawned on me that I was feeling a little better, but I just have to deal with Dean's death with the help of the lord. The treatments seemed to have helped some, but I was still going to the hospital because I wasn't dealing with Dean's death at all. When I got out of the hospital I went to my friend's house I saw a yellow envelope I knew it was the obituary his mother had sent me. I couldn't handle being at the house knowing it was there. So I left home. After a few weeks went by, I was able to finally go to my friend's house again and look at the obituary, it was nice. Only one thing bothered me besides seeing his pictures was that the woman he had been with for fifteen years name was on there. I had to think long and hard that he wasn't the one that wrote the obituary. I knew his heart was with me, so I got over it. I started to feel better after a while, when I would see his feet dancing I would say there goes Dean showing people in heaven his dance moves. It gets very hard sometimes I would fall apart when I see a roof that Dean fixed at my friend's house. I sometimes had to leave her house because instead of visiting I would find myself in a daze thinking about when I use to help Dean paint houses. I would even pass by a house that Dean put a roof on. If I was with someone I would say my Dean put the roof on that house. I wonder if I would ever get pass doing that. I certainly hope so. My heart hurts from the lost of my man. Dean rest in peace my love, Goodbye.

Chapter 22

I didn't know what to do with myself. After all this was the first time I was ever on my own, I didn't know where to begin. I knew I was on my way to becoming self destructive. I really didn't know what to do. To me, my life was meaningless. After I got out of the hospital I didn't want to face the world. One day I was so tired of living that I started to smoke crack. I had been sick for a long time that I thought that if I smoked crack cocaine that it would take away all of my problems and end my life. I just knew that with the illnesses that I had that smoking crack couldn't have agreed with me at all. A person that was not sick was dying from smoking. I had started to smoke often so I could get my life over with like a coward. I was so afraid of just ending it by taking a bottle of pills. I was too afraid of just jumping in front of a car that I just depended on crack cocaine to kill me. I had thought of so many ways of killing myself but I was really afraid of the Lord not forgiving me. I sometimes prayed that I would never wake up. I was at the worse stage of my life that I was wishing anything would happen to me. Sometimes I would rush to the hospital if I began to feel suicidal. I was in a do or die situation. Sometimes I wanted to die and then again I wanted to live. Dying was my first choice most of the time.

I had to be admitted to the hospital again. When I got out the hospital I was ok for a little while. Then my mind focused on my Dean so much that I wanted to become numb to the world around me. So I went over to Stephanie's house. Stephanie was an out cold girl; she didn't care about what she did or who with. Anyway I began to hang out with her all the time. I didn't know she was in love with women and men, with no shame about it. She thought I was an easy prey. She soon found out she was very wrong. Stephanie had so many girlfriends and boyfriends, they mostly knew each other, and she was always the drama queen on the block. She stayed into it with everyone she knew. Stephanie loved to be in anything that had to do with trouble.

I started smoking crack cocaine more often when I started to hang around with Stephanie. Stephanie took me to this house where all they did was sold and smoked crack. It was a very dangerous situation to be in. The house was always getting raided and shot at. But as long as I got some crack cocaine I didn't care. The only thing that I was uncomfortable about was all the women that were fighting over me. I didn't care how much I let them know that I didn't go for women, the harder they attempted to chase after me. Stephanie thought since I was over there with her she has some pull over me. Ha, I don't think so, well I know "not." I had to cut her off for awhile before things got out of hand.

The house we were at was very popular. Everyone knew about it. I met this girl that I called Ms. Wichita, because she had had mostly everyone she came in contact with, no matter if it was a male or female, white or black. Ms. Wichita didn't care what she would do for anything. If a person wanted to run a train on her she would be ready. She was ready before they could say anything else. Her body was so beaten up from so much sex and all the different toys she would carry around that she was walking like she was on a horse. Ms. Wichita was even more out colder than Stephanie was by a long ways. Ms. Wichita would get some of the handsomest rich white men. They were crazy about her," go figure". I just couldn't understand that. She was kind of pretty but she had been with so many people that she started to look a lot older than she was. Ms. Wichita was known as the woman that any man or woman could get. There was no hold barred with her. I knew this drug dealer that asked all the females about this man that would let him have sex with her for five hundred dollars if he could have sex with her in the butt. Ms. Wichita jumped up so fast I thought there was a fire; she went and made that money. The white man liked her so much that he became her regular customer. He was a married man and he had a lot to lose. Ms. Wichita got that man hooked on drugs. From that day on, he provided crack cocaine for everyone in the house. After awhile Ms. Wichita got mad at him and called his wife and his job as an architect to tell them he was on drugs. And guess what his wife divorced him and he lost his job. I felt so sorry for him that I never liked her much from that day on. I do hope and pray that she gets herself together and go and take care of her children that someone else is raising. That man is now homeless. He loss everything he had worked hard for. As a matter of fact she has got a lot of white men fired from their jobs and divorced. She was always out to get someone that decided to move on without her so she took revenge out on them and their families. They say she has done a lot of men like that. Well they are the real ones to blame that was their choice. No one else could make them do that but themselves. Ms. Wichita thought she could get me with her crack cocaine but she was so wrong. I had my own money and drugs each time I went over to the dope house, everyone was after me big time. The women were at me faster than the men, I had never been through that before. I really didn't know how to react. The only thing I could say was that I was not into women. But each and every time I went over there it was always the same thing. I started to get in good with them in case I needed something. It was so much violence around that the women always protected me. One day I asked the owner about the way those women were about me. He said that I was new meat and they were trying to knock out the competition. I said to him I don't like women so what do you mean about that statement? He said they don't know if they could get you or not, but they were not about to lose in the game. I said to him there wasn't a chance. He said again they are holding a bet to see who could get me first. He said just let them keep on thinking and I would get all the crack I wanted. So I went on to let them think what they wanted to. After awhile I just stopped going over there because they were too adamant about getting me that I saw trouble brewing up. Don't get me wrong, I am not judging anyone by any means, all the things I have done myself, but I just wasn't into going with women. I love people no matter what. I can be best friends with anyone. A friend is a friend no matter what. So I just stopped going over there often. I would stop by to see how the owner was doing when I was in the neighborhood.

After getting bored at staying home so much an associate of mine came by and asked me to go to her cousin's house with her so I did. When I went in the house, immediately one of her cousins fell in love with me. I kind of liked him to. I began to spend a lot of time over there. It was also a hang out but my friend made it clear that I was there to see him, so I didn't have that problem over there. Tom was his name. Tom had an uncle that stayed there also. Tom knew mostly all the people that came over there had a crush on me but they knew their place. Over there I sold crack and smoked it at the same time. My biggest customer was a financially well off white man; he was very nice when I saw him. I did hate that he was on drugs; he had so much to lose. He would buy a lot of crack from me, which is the reason I could always set up the house with crack. I think that was the only reason they loved to see me coming. When you have some crack on you all kinds of people would become your friend. You wouldn't believe all the friends you will make. Because I had the crack they were all around me like a bad yeast infection in the night time.

I would always look nice. I would always have a pretty seductive dress on. I had my make-up on. I always had some shoes on that every woman in there wanted, probably just to sell to get some crack.

I used to keep my nails done every two weeks. I always had a bundle of cash and drugs on me somewhere. I used to be the life of the crack party. What an honor for a fool.

I became associates with this older lady named Shelia. Shelia was a very lovely sophisticated and classy lady. She was very beautiful and she could out dance almost any young girl. Shelia also smoked crack and sold it too. I had never seen a lady that smoked crack with so much class. Shelia would watch over me like a big sister. I love Shelia for being there for me and giving me advice about stopping crack even if it didn't work, she tried anyway. She used to give me advice about men.

I had to go to the hospital Shelia would come and visit and bring me things like pajamas and whatever I needed. If for some reason I was out of crack I always had good credit with some drug dealers, so not having drugs was not an issue. I stayed in good standing with my drug dealers. I had an account with Mexicans, blacks and whites there was no problem with not having any drugs.

When I used to be at home by myself, I would get bored so I would sit in my bed. I would think of all kinds of flavored crack. I would soak my crack in tequila over night and use different flavored kool aid for flavor. I would experiment with brandy and cognac to make it more potent. I didn't like the flavors it came in. Anyway, I changed the flavor; it was just as deadly if not more.

There was always a place I never should have ever been. I stayed at a sleazy motel to sell some drugs from the motel room not knowing when the police was going to bust in, because it was a motel known for selling drugs. After weeks of staying there, I went back to my home. I received a call saying the motel room I was staying in had just got raided. I left the motel room just in time by the grace of God. My associate I left there was arrested, I was happy I was not there or I would have been in the same boat as him. I never needed to have a drug charge on top of a domestic charge.

Each and every time something happened I would have just left and that place was raided. That lets me know that I was protected by

God. There was no other reason behind all this but I continued to mess things up. I had more freedom to smoke crack and do whatever I wanted too.

I thought I was the queen of the crack world because I could stop whenever I wanted to. I didn't understand that. I watched people walking the streets trying to sell any and every thing from their bodies and their children also. They would sell anything they could get for a dime. People used to come to me and ask if they could buy a dollar worth of crack. I always felt sorry for them so I wouldn't take the dollar I would just give it to them. The white man kept me supplied with so much crack, that I would get bored with it and not touch it for a few weeks or months

I was propositioned by so many men and women because I had money and crack. I was acting so sophisticated. I had two to three long Pyrex crack pipes that were hardly ever empty. I really didn't like crack I was just doing anything that would numb the depression I was going through, it only made things worse.

One day I was at an associate's house, I had been smoking crack all day. I had become very tired so I took some anxiety medicine. I took the pills before I went to sleep. Before I went to sleep I called myself hiding my three hundred dollars in the pillow case I was sleeping on.

When I woke up the guy that owned the house was gone and so was my three hundred dollars. As I waited on him to come back he never did, so I decided to go home. I saw some blood on the front steps. It didn't faze me much but I was wondering why he would leave me alone in his house so long. I kept going over there to see what had happened. A week later I found out he had went to get some drugs with my money and the man that took him to get drugs was expecting to get some drugs for taking him to the dealer. See what had happened was the man that owned the house wouldn't give him any drugs so he got upset and sliced his throat on the front porch. I was sleeping hard that I was lucky that I didn't wake up at the time, or I may not have lived to see this day. That's why

I couldn't find him; he was in the hospital fighting for his life. He didn't get a chance to smoke the crack he stole my money for.

A few months later I saw him. I asked him how he was doing. He said ok but he was dealing with his throat being sliced. I wanted so bad to ask him did he have that three hundred dollars but I just left it alone. He was paying for it big time.

At that same house that day he was in the same room having sex with another man. Since I had been in the drug world there was a lot to see, women having sex with women. They had threesomes and doing any and everything to each other to get a hit of crack. I have saw men performing oral sex with women. I remember one day this one girl introduced me to this tall buffed handsome man, I was digging him a little. He took me out to dinner. He would hold conversations with me on the phone for hours. He and I got alone very well until this particular night we were lying on the bed watching television. He began to kiss me; it was nice in the beginning. Then he began to get ruff with me. When I would say stop, he would get even more persistent, then when I pushed him away with all the strength I had. He started saying all these strange things like, oh you are too good for me? I would say no, I just wasn't ready for that right now. He was calling me all kinds of things like bitch you are going to give me some of this pussy. I was fighting him as hard as I could. He was really scaring me big time. When he almost got to do what he was trying to do one of the girls I knew was knocking on the door. I screamed loud for her to come in. He put his hand over my mouth then he said when he takes his hand off my mouth I better not scream. I said to him she has a key to my house because she was visiting so much that I got tired of getting up to open the door for her. When he was almost where he wanted to be I said to him that my friend was going to come in. If I had a sticky note on the mailbox she knew not to come in at all. I was thankful that I didn't have a sticky note on the mailbox. He said no she couldn't get in because the door was locked. I told him that she had a key to the house. He said stop lying. After a few more seconds she used the key, she was only supposed to come in if I didn't answer the door in a few minutes. That was the first time I was so happy to see her. When he jumped off of me I hurried to the living room. I guess I was looking to suspicious because she asked me what was wrong. I said nothing, she said yes there is. She asked him what was wrong with me, he said nothing. She knew he had done something because she knew how I was, I would have said something smart to her or played a trick on her, but this time I was not doing anything. She called me in the bathroom and told me that she needed to know what he had done to me. So I went on and told her he tried to force me to have sex with him. When I told her that, she went to the kitchen to get a knife. Then she went in the living room and told him to leave and now. As he was walking out the door he said he would see me later. When he said that, there was tightness in the pit of my stomach. That night was terrifying. I was so scared. I was calling some women that I knew so they would come over to spend the night. I had a knife everywhere I could get to it quick. I even called the neighbor for him to keep watch on my house because he is always up and being nosey anyway. I was so afraid that I didn't let anyone of the girls let their boyfriends in my house. It was so bad that I didn't let any man in my house for a few weeks. I didn't understand why I didn't want any man in my house. They could have protected me but I was afraid of all men for a few weeks.

Being in the crack world you would see almost everything. I had been around that type of stuff that I became used to seeing all kinds of sex acts. It was nothing for someone to steal in front of you without blinking an eye. I have learned more in my three years in Wichita than I had in the first forty years of my life.

One day I was sitting around with my friend Linda. The both of us had a pocket full of crack we were sitting down smoking. There were a lot of people around that didn't have any crack or money. The owner of the house would throw people out. He used to say if you crack heads don't have any money or crack they could get the hell out. He was the head crack smoker himself, I was sitting down with two pipes in my hand, it dawned on me that I was also a crack head. I became so embarrassed to myself that I stopped smoking. I had some money and crack, but I was no more special than that man they called a crack head. I didn't like that name "crack head." I really believe if it wasn't for GOD I would not have been here to tell my story.

GOD was there for me but I still was not faithful to him like I should have been. I not only think about me putting myself in danger but the people I supplied the crack to, there was this white man that was very cool. I liked how nice he was. I used to go to his house in another small city about fifteen minutes away from where I lived. If he wanted some crack I would go to his house so he could have company while he smoked. He didn't like to be by himself when he was smoking. I didn't smoke I just kept him company. I had stopped smoking but I still sold it for a few more weeks and I stopped even doing that.

I loved his home it had a Jacuzzi and a underground swimming pool. When I went over to his house I had the run of it because he stayed up stairs when he smoked. He would always have me everything I needed so I didn't have to leave quickly. Sometimes I used to stay the whole night over there. He had a job at one of those aircraft companies.

The girl I told you about earlier Ms. Wichita got so jealous of me because I had that connection that she called the aircraft company to report that he was a drug user. He told me that when he got to his fancy office that there were two officers there waiting for him so he could respond to the allegation against him, they asked him to take a drug test. He had no choice but to take the test. Of course he failed. Because his job was so important they gave him a chance to go to a rehab center. I really felt bad about what that trifling hooker did to him and even more families. That's the price some people have to pay when they go outside of their own home for some trick that didn't give a damn about nothing but the crack.

I had to keep my mind focused on something other than the crack. I had to do something with my life. I decided after that last incident I knew it was time to make a change. The crack world was just a big dangerous circle going around and around. I stopped dealing with all that madness and moved back to Michigan to get away from that madness and self destruction.

Chapter 23

Time was passing by fast like the world was rushing by for the time of our Lord to ascend again. Everyone was in a rush to get to no place. I was the main one trying to go. The thing was I wasn't ready for the LORD to come. I knew I better stop procrastinating. I am rushing to get this book published; hoping to help someone to get some help before it's too late and all those bad things piled up on you and cause you to snap in the worse way.

It has been eight months since my Dean passed on. One day when I was over my friend's house one of her nephew's came over to visit. His name was the same as my Dean's so I will call him Dean II. We were sitting on the couch just reminiscing about the past. I said to Dean II do you remember when you had a crush on me? Dean II just smoothly let me know he was not a boy anymore, we just laughed for a long time. Dean II was so sweet and such a delight to have around, and how he loved the LORD. Whenever you saw Dean II he was always giving a shout out to the LORD. Dean II taught the word of the LORD with such passion and love.

When I got married Dean II sang the song here and Now by Luther Vandross as I walked down the aisle. Dean II would sing his praises to the LORD and made everyone stand on their feet rejoicing the LORD right along with him.

It was Christmas season. Everyone was getting ready to rejoice in the name of the LORD. Everyone was having a good time but that good time was short lived. Tragedy struck without a warning as it did with my Dean. My friend's nephew was found in his house on the floor from a fatal heart attack. I just didn't understand why the LORD would take one of his disciples away from us, then it dawn on me why not take him out of this crazy world. Dean II was ready for the LORD I am sure of that.

When we got the call about Dean II being dead, I felt like I was in another world. I started to think of my Dean all over again. I loved my play nephew so much I thought I was at the end of my rope all over again.

My two Dean's was gone a few months apart. So much was going wrong in my life that I wanted to die myself. But the good LORD wasn't ready for me yet, I do believe the LORD was waiting for me to get myself in order.

Chapter 24

A few months has gone passed since my special nephew died. It was the anniversary of my Dean's deaths. I didn't know how I was going to deal with this day. I knew the closer that day came the more I became deeply depressed, I needed to do something to get pass this day.

The day had finally come; it has been exactly one year that my Dean passed on. I had that same feeling again that I had just been told my Dean was dead. The bad feeling was consuming me.

Everything was coming down on me. My depression was so bad that I had to call my friend to come and find me. I was just walking around not knowing where I was going just crying, not knowing where I was at or where I lived. I remember my friends cell phone number was programmed in my phone. I called her and told her the street names and she came to pick me up. I didn't know I was just a few blocks from my house. If you don't get any help you can lose your mind. Without your mind you have lost yourself. Your mind is you. I can't stress this enough, get help! You don't want to end up in a world of mess because you just don't care about anything, and not caring about anything you will do anything that is not the normal you.

It happened to be the week of my church convention in Detroit Michigan. I was not going to go because I was in such a bad state of mind. I just wanted to be left alone to go through whatever I had to go through. My friend refused to let me be alone. An hour before it was time for everyone to be going, all of a sudden I knew I might not be here when she got back, so I rushed to pack my clothes. At that time I guess I wanted to live.

We had finally made it to the church. I was listening to the sermon closely hoping that someone would say a powerful word or something to save me from myself and my weakness of letting the devil get me tangled all up. As I was listening to the testimonies, I tried not to fall apart in front of everyone. I was listening to a lot more testimonies. I had to think that I needed to get it together. I knew I was a different person with different problems so I had to think of how to deal with my own self hold ups. I was giving different problems to work with so I had to focus on myself and pray for other people's problems other than my own.

There was no better place to let out all of the bad things I had gone though, but I was too bashful to speak up. It was a little easier to testify in my own church than someone else's church.

I needed GOD so bad, LORD please help me to cope with this demon that's trying to fight against me to stop me from getting close to you LORD. I do believe you will heal me from all this depression and all these other Illnesses. I pray in your loving name! Amen.

Chapter 25

I was ready for the next step. I hope and pray that the journey of my life would be a lot different, but then again maybe not. I had to do something positive with my life. I needed something to focus on.

I have always had a problem with my weight. I had decided to join a health club for the, I don't know how many times. I always loved to walk on the treadmill. If I had a walkman to listen to, I would walk for miles. I never accomplished much of anything if I didn't have any music to listen to.

I always liked to go to the gym early in the morning like about seven, then afterwards I would go back home and go back to bed and rest for an hour or so. I would always feel better after a workout. On one morning I got up feeling pretty good, I just knew this morning something good was going to happen. I got up from my bed and got dressed for the gym.

I was doing my usual workout on the treadmill listening to my favorite singer Otis Redding singing those love songs when I happen to glance to the right of me. I saw this tall handsome muscle bound delicious looking man. We seem to have been looking into each other's eyes at the same time. I quickly turned my head. I was hoping I would not trip on my own feet and go flying backwards falling on my butt. I tend to get very nervous around my black men for some strange reason. When I would be around white men it didn't bother me at all, go figure.

As I continued walking I was thinking I hope I don't fall down. I was making myself more nervous. I wanted to turn and get another look but I was afraid he might be looking at me. I at least hope so. I finally got up enough nerves to turn my head to look his way. When I did look at him he was looking so good with his sweaty body. He was lifting weights and sweating profusely. He had the most beautiful biceps and triceps I had seen in a long time. I was trying hard not to fly off the treadmill while being nosey watching this fine man. I almost tripped when he turned his head my way. I hurried and turned my head hoping that he didn't notice that I was looking at him. I continued to walk and pretend I was not looking at him. About ten minutes later I was looking at him through the mirror when I saw him looking my way. I saw him getting closer and closer. It looked like he was coming my way. As he was getting closer, I was getting more and more nervous. After a few more seconds he finally made it to me. I was saying please don't fall. He said with a heavy masculine bass voice "hi Miss Lady." I responded with a soft trimming soprano voice hello sir how are you? He said he was doing just fine. Then he said his name was Michael. I told him my name was Lagretto. Then he started to strike up a conversation. He said he comes to the gym five times a week but he had never seen me there before. I said I had just joined the gym. Then he asked me if I was married, I said no, and how about you, he said he has never been married before. I asked him why not, he said he had never found the woman that he wanted to spend his life with. Then he asked me if I had a man? I said no. I asked what about you do you have a lady friend, he said no. I wanted to shout but I had to keep my composure and act like a lady. I was trying not to make a fool of myself. Then he said if he asked me would I do him the honor of having dinner with him what would I say? I said ask me and find out. He then said Miss Lady, will you have dinner with me on Saturday? I said,

I would be delighted to have dinner with you. He then gave me his phone number. He gave me a cell phone number and a house number. That was good he gave me his house number, I would hope that that meant he didn't have a lady. I didn't know these men had gotten so bolted these days they could be talking to you with their woman next to them. I learned that in Wichita. He then said he would be waiting for me to call so we could work out the details. I said ok and it was a pleasure meeting him. Then he went on his way. I know I was happy I didn't go flying across the room.

Chapter 26

It has been three days since I met Michael. I didn't want to call him too quickly. I didn't want him to think I was desperate for a man which I was. I decided to call him after a few days. I was tired of torturing myself. I dialed his house phone number first. When I dialed the number I had got so nervous that I wished I could hang up but it was too late. After a few seconds I heard a soft voice on the phone saying hello. I knew it was not Michael. I then asked if I could speak to Michael. The soft voice on the phone asked who was calling. I said Lagretto; the soft voice replied back and asked me to hold on. After about thirty seconds a masculine voice said hello. I then said hello Michael this is Lagretto, he said he knew. I just thought I was going to pass out. Michael asked what happened to me and him having dinner together. He then asked would I have dinner with him tonight. I said how about I invite you over to my house tomorrow for a home cooked meal; he said that would be even better. I then said I need to be going, I would call you later. I really didn't want to get off the phone, but then again I didn't want to seem desperate. As soon as I got off the phone I wanted to kick myself, I knew I had to go to the store and I had to clean the house. I wish I had thought about this before I opened my big mouth, but it was too late. I had to decide what I was going to cook for dinner, perhaps a steak a baked potato and a side salad. I was planning a meal that would keep him coming back for more. I had to decide what I was going to wear; all my clothing was old fashion. I will just have to go out and buy something new. As the time was getting closer I began to get nervous. I didn't want to mess things up. I needed to slow down. I had a whole day to plan and prepare for. I grabbed my keys and coat and I went to the clothing store first, I saw this beautiful lavender dress that would be perfect. I needed to buy a good supporting bra. I have always had big breast that I hate but men, they love them. For me it would have been nice if I could have gotten a little less breast and more butt and hips. I bought everything new even down to the stockings. I lucked up and found the perfect pair of lavender shoes.

I was all set with what I was going to wear. Now I needed to get my hair and nails done. After doing all that I was ready to get to the grocery store. I was running around like a chicken with his head cut off. I was so tired, I wondered if I would be any good when Michael gets here. I needed to get a good night's rest; I was so excited I couldn't sleep. My nerves were getting the best of me. I got out of the bed I begin to clean what I hadn't finished. I wanted to make everything perfect. I hoped that he would like everything. It was now morning. Everything was nice, I recorded a CD of soft love songs to set the mood, and I wanted it warm and soothing. The bait was set I was ready to reel him in; all I needed now was for him to catch on. I was ready for some good love making tonight. I know I should not give it up on the first date but I was in despair and in need of some affection, and I was going to get it that night. When he started to hit on me I would appear to be uninterested, after all a lady has to do what a lady has to do, and then there comes a time when she can get a little freaky, and the time was then.

Michael was to be at my house at seven o'clock, it was now two thirty. I set the table the night before when I was unable to sleep. I set the alarm for eight a.m. I wanted to start my preparation of the food so that I would be able to start dinner at a time where it could be as fresh as possible. I wanted everything cooked and set up for Michael when he arrived. When Michael gets here we could sit at the table and begin to eat as soon as possible. I had the perfect dress a little sexy but not to revealing, sassy but classy. I wore some 3" pumps. I wanted everything perfect. I tend to get nervous around men like I said before. I hoped I wouldn't trip on my own feet when he gets here.

Now it was time for Michael to arrive. I had to make my last mirror check. As I was admiring myself there was a knock at the door. I asked who it was, a masculine voice said Michael. When I opened the door I could feel my heart beating fast. There was this six foot tall man with broad shoulders he looked good in his purple suit. He came in the house. He said that I looked very lovely. I thanked him. Michael said it looked like we planned to wear those colors.

I told him everything was ready. I asked him if he was ready to eat. He said yes. I showed him where the bathroom was so that he could wash his hands. Michael said everything looked very good, I hoped it taste as good as it looked, he said he was sure it would.

As I was getting ready to sit down at the table he pulled my chair out for me, which was a plus on his part. I enjoyed listening to him as he began to say the grace over the dinner that was another plus for him. I enjoyed the look on his face each time he took a bite of food I could see he was enjoying his meal. My bait food consisted of collard greens, sweet potatoes, hot water cornbread, and corn on the cob and baked barbecue chicken. For dessert I cooked peach cobbler, Michael said that was his favorite dessert. I told him I really didn't have a favorite dessert I like peach cobbler, blue berry cobbler, banana pudding, German Chocolate cake and caramel cake. All of those were equally as good as the next. Michael said that was a wide variety of favorite desserts, I said I know. Michael and I talked about everything at the kitchen table. We talked about pass relationships. Michael had already told me that he wasn't married. I was wondering what the real reason he had never been married. All of this was too good to be true. Michael said he had come close a few times. I asked him what happened. He said that he guess he wasn't ready for marriage at that time. I asked him what about now. I wanted to take it back; I told him I was sorry and too forget that question. He said it was fine. He then said he thinks he has grown enough in wisdom that he was ready for marriage with a person that is settled and ready for him. I wanted to shout. I was feeling good when he told me he is ready for marriage. He just didn't know how that made me feel. I needed to stop there with the married thing. I didn't want to push him away. Michael began to ask me about my past marriage. I was so embarrassed about the question, I just told him that I was married once but my marriage was a disaster. Michael asked me what happened. I wish he had not asked me anything about that part of my life. Those are memories I didn't care to bring back. I guess I had to start this relationship off right if I wanted it to get serious with this man without having skeletons in my closet. I shared the least little information I could with Michael that I was comfortable with sharing. I told him I was married once to a man that was terrible, and that he mentally and physically abused me. Michael said he was sorry about that. I said it was ok; it's in my past, but thank you. Then he asked me to tell him about myself. I told him I was born in Arkansas and that I had moved to Michigan because I needed to get away from the nightmares in my life. I told him I was sold to my parents when I was a baby in a baby selling ring and that I found that out when I was fifteen years old. I let him know that my parents were in prison because of the baby buying. Michael was in shock to hear such a story. I really didn't like to talk about that much. I asked Michael if he needed to know anymore. He said if it really hurt me that much just to leave it alone. He was more concerned about here and now, I thanked him for understanding. That was a load off my mine.

Michael was so very nice. I hoped it wasn't all just a put on. The food was ready. It was time for us to eat. I was enjoying Michael; I had not had anyone to hold an interesting conversation with since my Dean was here.

Michael said he had not had a meal like that since his mothers cooking. I thanked him. I could tell that Michael was enjoying himself.

When we were done eating Michael and I went into the living room to talk. The both of us were good and full. I must say that was a good meal. The mood was soothing and romantic. I had put on some Teddy Pendergrass and when Teddy was playing you couldn't help but to get in the mood. I was already horny as could be. I was thinking maybe I should have just turn that type of music off. I didn't want him to know I was ready to jump him, throw him down and give him a workout he would never forget. I was feeling Michael quite a bit. As I went to change the music to Barry White, Michael said that was his type of music. I told him I like mostly blues and slow music and some reggae. Michael was impressed with my music collection. I even put on some Al Green. Now who can resist Al's music, not me and I hoped neither could he. I didn't want him to think I was easy. I was really beginning to like him a lot; I didn't want to scare him off. If Michael starts to get fresh I would try to distract him, I was just a human. I could only take so much. If he started to kiss me I might have melted all over him. I didn't want to get freaky on the first date. I wanted to get laid bad but I had to carry myself like a lady.

If it was just a casual thing I would have already jumped him. As for getting laid, I just might have, but this was a person that I was trying to get to know. In other words, I liked Michael enough that I didn't want to run him off. I did not want him to think that I was coming on too strong.

Michael was talking about the things he had accomplished at this stage of his life. Michael said he went to a private school until he graduated. He said he graduated from Western Michigan University with a master's Degree in Criminal Justice and that he was a parole officer. And he was a counselor for the prison. I was very impressed. I didn't want to tell this man, I didn't have a job and I was on disability for major depression and that I had a Medicare and Medicaid card. I was too embarrassed at not doing anything with my life. Was I supposed to tell this man that I had been on drugs and that I prostituted myself? I began to feel worthless. I told Michael that his job sounded interesting.

I asked Michael what was the most exciting incident he had ever had on the job? Michael said there was once an inmate that was angry about a report he had to write on him trying to stab him with this homemade knife. I asked him what he did. Michael said he had to wrestle him to the floor. I asked what they did to the inmate. Michael said they added ten years on with the charge he already had. Michael said he only had two more years to go. Otherwise, he would have been home now if he wouldn't have tried to shank him. Michael said that the man was so used to confinement that he didn't want to leave prison. He did that so he wouldn't have to leave. Michael also said the man was gay and that it was easier for him to be with men in lock up than it was in the free world.

I had already heard about that before. I didn't think that a person would prefer being caged to freedom. I said what ever worked for them. I had never been in that situation before, so I was on the outer looking in.

Michael was sitting there next to me looking good and smelling delightful. I had a hard time controlling myself. I really needed to change the sound to something less than love music. Who could resist Keith Sweat and Teddy Pendergrass, I know I couldn't much longer. Michael was seducing me with his charm. The way he held my hand was like he was deliberately trying to make me lose the little self control I had left. Michael was not playing fair. His body was calling my name, but I had to contain myself if I wanted him to respect me the same after. I almost didn't care for a minute. I really did need to focus on something else. I asked Michael could we watch TV for a little while, he said that it would be ok with him. I went to turn the music off and turn the television on. I made sure I found something like a western or drama show, you know, something that would get both of our minds tuned to something other than love making.

I asked Michael did he want a drink. He said no, that he didn't drink much and he had never smoked a cigarette before. He said he would only drink casually. That was a big plus for him. I had been around so much of that that I didn't really want anyone around me that smoked or drank. Everything about Michael was too good to be true. When would I find the true Michael Watts? Would he turn out to be a woman? All kinds of negative things kept going through my mind like maybe he was a killer or a baby molester. I hope he was on the up and up, because I was really feeling him.

I was having a good time since I turned off that seductive music. I wished the night would never end. Every minute of being with him made me feel good all over. After hours of torture Michael said he was sorry but he had to get going. He had to be at work at seven in the morning. I was sorry and relieved at the same time. I was happy because if he wouldn't have said he had to go I would have given in sooner or later. I was in need of some love and soon. I walked Michael to the door. He said he would call me tomorrow on his breaks. Then he gave me this kiss that was so passionate and tender that I wanted to pull him back in the house and love him to the limit. Well I didn't, so he went to his car while I was acting like a little kid watching him with my lips poked out because I really didn't want him to go. I shut the door and went back to the living room to finish watching the show Michael and I was watching.

I didn't get much sleep. I kept visioning Michael sitting on the couch with his clothes off. I thought about Michael most of the night until I fell asleep around five A.M. It was eight in the morning the phone rang. I was still very tired. But when I heard the nice masculine voice of Michael I quickly woke up. That phone call was a nice wake up call. I tried not to sound too excited about Michael calling but I must say that I was smiling from ear to ear. I said good morning and how are you doing on this beautiful morning?

He said just lovely after visioning my beautiful smile. Michael asked me how I was. I told him I was doing just fine. Michael said he was at work but he needed to call. I would invite him over again. I said well I do thank you and that I enjoyed his company and would like him to come over after work to have dinner with me. Michael said he would much rather take me out to dinner because I had cooked him such a nice dinner last night that he wanted to do something to show me how he appreciated the time I had put into preparing such a beautiful dinner. I told him I would be delighted. Then he said he would call me on his lunch break. I said ok then he said I'll talk to you later then we said good bye. After I hung up the phone I was dancing and jumping almost to the ceiling with excitement.

I needed to go through my closet to see what I had to wear. I knew now that I needed to go shopping to get new clothes. I saw that Michael liked to go out and I didn't want to be an embarrassment to him. At this time I was not able to afford anymore new clothes just yet. In the mean time I would just mix and match something together.

I had been looking for something to wear for a few hours and had not found anything that I liked. One of my associates said that I am so self conscious about my looks, I knew she was right. I had been that way since I was with my ex-husband. Dealing with so much mental abuse being called fat bitches and no one else would want me.

Michael did call on his lunch break like he said he would, unlike most "men". I asked him what type of restaurant we were going to, he said to this new barbeque place down town. I told him I needed to know so I would know what to wear. Michael said that I could just wear some jeans. That took a load off my mind. Michael said that he would be over to pick me up at six. I told him I would be ready, and then we said good-bye. I really didn't want to wear any blue jeans but since Michael said I could wear jeans, I put on a pair with a dressy blouse and some heals. That would be ok. My hair was already done from yesterday; I just had to put on my makeup.

It was time for Michael to be here. I was just more nervous, if not even more than I was yesterday, maybe because I was not at my own house. I heard someone knocking on the door. It was Michael ten minutes early but that was ok. I had to do my last mirror check. I had to make sure it was not any toilet paper on the bottom of my shoe or some other crazy thing that had happened to me before.

I went to the door and asked who it was, that base tone voice said Michael? I opened the door and looked in the face of that handsome man. Michael was looking mighty good. Michael said that I was looking very pretty. I thanked him.

Michael knew about this nice restaurant down town. Then he asked me do I mind going to dinner with him to a restaurant on the water front instead of that barbeque place? I said no I don't mind. I asked Michael would I need to change into something dressier than the clothes I had on. He said no that I was looking good enough to bypass eating out, and then he laughed. I had to change the subject quickly. I asked him what the name of the restaurant was. He said The Shae' Lorrince. I told him that I heard about that restaurant before and that was a very expensive place, he said yes it was. Well I said to myself that he already knows how expensive the restaurant was, he still wanted to take me. I guess we would be on our way, so we left. I forgot that whoever told me about the restaurant said you have to make a reservation. I asked Michael, he said yes, he knew and for me to stop worrying about anything that he had everything under control. I said to myself, this man is too good to be true.

Just before we pulled out of the driveway it popped in my head that I was not dressed for that type of restaurant, Michael said I looked lovely. I still was not content so, Michael said if I would feel more comfortable that maybe I needed to change but he thought I look good. I rushed back in the house to change.

Michael was looking so nice I just wanted to wear something dressier. While I was getting ready I told Michael to have something to drink while I got dressed. I was so nervous trying to find me something to wear. I couldn't be in a fancy place, with what I had on. Michael was dressed dressy. I asked him why he didn't call to let me know that we were going to such a fine restaurant. Michael said that's was why he came a little early so if I wanted to change we would not be late for our reservation. Michael said that when he said how good I looked that he just didn't feel the need to tell me I needed to change. That was very nice of Michael.

I finally found a nice dress that I would be ok with after junking up my bedroom, I came out. Michael was impressed, he said wow. With his reaction I guess he must have been pleased. Michael said I looked so beautiful. Thank you, I said. I then said I was ready to go, and we went out to the car. I asked Michael were we late? He said no we were ok.

Michael opened the door for me then he said, that a gentleman supposed to open doors for a lady. Then he made another statement that when we are out in public that he didn't want me to open any doors. Then he said that when we stop that he would come to my side to open the door for me. Michael also said that when we get to the door at the restaurant to wait on him so he can open the door for me. Michael sure did have a lot of instructions for me; he also said I am to wait for him to pull out the chair for me. Then I went to thinking that this is too good to be true, for real now. I thought this man must have been a controlling nut. I was making it seem like I didn't want a man to do those things for me but it was not like that. I just didn't think that he was on the up and up. I know I should hope that there are still a few gentlemen that exist today. I was so used to men doing everything but being a gentleman, that I just didn't think I would meet another one. I had been with a man that might open the door if they were already next to it, and that is taking it a little too far even then. The only other real gentleman I had was Dean. It just popped in my mind that what if I start to compare other men to my Dean, Lord that seems to be what I am doing.

When we got to the restaurant Michael got out the car and came around to my side and opened the door and took my hand, like he said he would. I had to be dreaming. When we walked in the restaurant

I saw the women with fancy dresses on. I was so glad that I changed clothes. If I had not changed I would have been so embarrassed. The restaurant was beautiful; it had a large lovely water fall. There were real napkins and not the paper napkins. I didn't drink much, but I told the waiter that I wanted what that lady had at that table that was next to us. When the waiter came back with my drink I tasted it. It was the best drink I had ever had. It was called a brandy Alexander. Michael had a glass of champagne. I most definitely had never had a man that would drink champagne. This man seemed to be out of my league. I only had one drink because I was not a real drinker and I didn't want to scare him off by acting a fool if I drank too much.

The restaurant was nice and I had fun. The Restaurant had a live band performing. The mood was very romantic. The waiters that came to our table and asked were we ready to order? I looked at Michael; he said we needed a little more time. After sitting there for a while I said I was ready. I ordered a prime rib medium well and baked potato and a salad. Michael told the waiter that he would have the lobster. Now I knew something was wrong with this man, Lobster, come on now, be for real. I am out with a killer what else could it be?

I loved prime rib; they are so succulent and tender. This restaurant was very nice, the females had on ties and a blue vest and white shirts and blue skirts. The males had on ties and a blue vest and white shirts and black slacks.

I had forgotten my anxiety medication. I was afraid that I might have an anxiety attack or a panic attack. I was worried that I was beginning to bring on an attack myself from thinking I might have one. I needed to focus on something else.

I had been having panic attacks every since my ex-husband mentally and physically abused me. I would have been so embarrassed if I have an attack in front of those people, especially around Michael. I had not told him about my medical problems, I was afraid that I would run him away if I have an attack in front of him. I hoped I could find an anxiety pill somewhere in my purse. Having anxiety and panic attacks can put a damper on the quality of my life and relationships. People just don't want to be bothered with someone else's problems.

The waiter brought us our salads first. A few minutes later he brought us our dinner. When I bit into my steak it was so juicy and tender that a toothless person could have easily eaten it without a problem. Everything was good. Michael loved his lobster.

The restaurant even had a dance floor and a live band. Michael had gotten up from the table after we were done eating and went over to the band. I saw him talking to the singer of the group. I didn't know what he was talking to them about though. After a few minutes the band started to play some Freddie Jackson's and Melba Moore's Just a little bit more. I love that song. Michael had requested that song for us to dance to. It was so nice when he came to me and asked could he have this dance, this man must be from a different planet. I told him I would be delighted. That song would get you in a lot of trouble or a lot of delight, either way I wanted it too. It felt so good to be in his arms. I wished there was an extended version of that song. I was really feeling this man. I hope he was feeling me too, anyway who can resist Freddie? Michael and I danced to a few more songs then we left the restaurant.

Michael also took me to a club. I was having such a good time. I had not had a good time for a while. I needed to pinch myself to see was I dreaming. We danced the night away. Michael knew a lot of the people at the club. He introduced me to a lot of his friends. They were very nice to me. After a few hours Michael took me home. Michael wanted to come in the house, but I couldn't trust myself. I was already hot and bothered. I told Michael I would see him later. He said ok and thanked me for the lovely time, I told him thank you for the best time I had had in a long time. Then he kissed me and said good night. I wanted him to come in so bad, but I will not be able to contain myself. After a few more dates I will let him come in the house. If I would have let him in, it would have been a hurricane

129

up in my house horny as I was. Michael would have been in danger. I know that when I do sleep with him he better be in good shape and have some triple A insurance. I will also need for him to sign a consent form that I will not be responsible for what may happen while engaging in sex; I did get a laugh out of that. It was good to laugh again and smile from being happy, even if it was just for a little while.

Michael and I had been spending a lot of time together. When we were not together we were on the phone all day and throughout the night. I was having a good time just talking to him on the phone. Michael and I had not made love yet and it had been three months since we started dating. A thought just went through my head that we were having so much fun that I was afraid that when we did make love that it would change a lot of things. I was afraid that he would be different towards me because he got what he wanted if we did sleep together too quickly. My ex-husband had done a job on me that I was afraid to get close to any man. I thought that because I was not giving him any that he may have found me challenging because I am hard to get. He doesn't know that I am hard to get because I like him for more than a little casual sex. I wonder if I do will he lose interest after it is not challenging anymore. I knew I shouldn't judge Michael by what another man did. I started to think about that all the time. I am fighting with myself about what I was going to do. I wanted and needed some love, like now. I am constantly thinking if I would be ok if the calls are less frequent. In past relationships I was ok with that because I didn't care because I was out for the same thing. I had developed this attitude that I would get them before they get me. I didn't want to be like that with Michael. I liked him very much. Michael was almost being too much of a gentleman. I was going to just have to take that chance.

Michael was coming over for dinner. I was going to cook some fish and spaghetti, some garlic toast and coleslaw. I didn't cook any dessert. Michael was thirty minutes late. That was ok because I had only seasoned the fish because I wanted it to be freshly cooked when he got here.

When Michael got to my house I started cooking the fish. We took our food to the living room so while we were eating we could be watching TV.

It was so nice to have Michael around. Michael and I had been hanging out so much that I was beginning to fall in love with him. I was not going to tell him that, not just yet. I was so happy being with Michael that I hoped I didn't mess it up because of what I had been through with past relationships.

Michael wanted me to put on some Keith Sweat. I thought to myself that was not a good thing. I was already horny as heck. I put it on any way. I was on dangerous territory with Michael and Keith. It wasn't fair two against one.

I was about to give in and jump him. I was tired of waiting, I wanted him now. Michael was too much of a gentleman. I wanted him to be a gentleman in the streets and a freaky thug in the bed room. He needed to have a little thug in him.

The atmosphere was so soothing and romantic. I noticed that Michael was trying not to show that he was in the mood for love. He was looking at me like he was trying to let me know that he was ready.

I'm sorry but as we were looking in each other eyes we were getting weaker and weaker, until we just couldn't hold out any longer. Michael took my hand and led me to the bedroom and started to make me feel like I was the only woman in the whole world, at least for that moment. The way he was making me feel, I accepted it.

Michael was kissing me in places I had not seen without a mirror. I was feeling so good. There was no other high that could compare to the way he made me feel. I would not change a thing. My body was getting a workout better than any gym could do. I felt like I needed to leave a tip on the night stand in my bedroom for a job "well" done. It was worth it and then some, a lot of some.

After Michael and I were done making love he held me in his arms, he made me feel special. I didn't know if I would ever see him again when he left but I would always have that special moment in my heart. Anyway what ever happen just happens. I was not going to worry about it.

I was just feeling good all over. It had been months of loving each other. Michael didn't leave me, he was still there loving me. Michael made our love making unforgettable each time we made love. I didn't know why but the love he was giving me was like the first time every time.

One day I was sitting around the house when Michael came over, he was such a delight to be with. I was in the living room watching T.V. he looked like he had something on his mind. I asked him what was wrong, he said nothing but he wanted to ask me something. I became so nervous I was hoping Michael was going to ask me to marry him, what else could he ask me?

Michael sat down beside me and looked in my eyes and said would I go with him on a trip to Trinidad to meet his parents? I was looking at him like I could have just slapped his face. I was glad he didn't know that I thought he was going to ask me to marry him. I told him I would love to go with him to meet his parents.

Michael asked me did I have a problem if we made it a vacation and went on a cruise to a few other exciting places. I told him that would be so much fun and sure I would love to.

I needed to go and get new clothes. I told Michael that I didn't have anything to wear on the trip. He said it was fine that he would take me shopping, I was very happy with that.

When we did go shopping Michael was spending money like it was free. Michael was talking like his parents were rich. I found out they were rich. I became very intimidated when Michael was talking about his parents. I was beginning to be afraid to go on this trip. I am afraid I am going to make a fool out of myself. I wanted to renege on going to meet his parents, but Michael was looking forward to me going so I didn't want to disappoint him.

The time was getting closer for us to go on the cruise. We were to leave in a few days; I was almost ready to go. I just needed to go and pick up a few things from the supply store. I needed more sun block and some earrings. I had my hair braided so I wouldn't have to worry about that.

Chapter 27

It's now time for us to be going. I had always been afraid of cruise ships. I was scared out of my mind. Michael asked me what was wrong. I told him that the ship was huge. He said it would be o.k. I said I know.

When we boarded the ship I was mesmerized by the size of the ship. It was elegant and classy. It had everything on it. Our room was a suite. It was filled with flowers and chocolate mints that were on the pillows. I had only seen chocolates on my bed when I stayed in a hotel in Las Vegas a life time ago. It was a dream to me. I couldn't believe where I was going.

Michael and I went to dinner in the ships dining room. We even went to a party on the ship, most of all we focused on each other.

When we made it to Trinidad I was speechless at how it looked. It was beautiful. I really didn't believe that there would be a limo to pick us up.

I was really afraid to meet his mother for some reason, maybe it's me. When we made it to their home it was a mansion. I was so amazed. When Michael said they were rich I thought he was saying they were not hurting for money. When I saw them they were rich for real. I found out that Michael was also rich. That explains a lot of the popularity and respect he got when he walked in a room. It had to sink in that I had a rich man.

Michael's parents were elegant. His mother walked with grace and class. His father was in a smoking jacket. They were o.k. until his mother opened her mouth. When Michael introduced me to his father he was nice and handsome. When he introduced me to his mother I knew right then and there I was in trouble. His mother said hi in a voice that let me know right away she didn't like me. I was hoping that I wouldn't have to put her in her place or she put me in mine.

We all talked but his mother was trying not to acknowledge me. His father was holding a conversation with me. But that mother of his, well let's just say if you can't say anything good don't say anything at all, so I'm going to try really, really, really hard to say nothing.

While we were at the dinner table Michael said to his parents he came to see them because he wanted to ask me something. I wanted to believe he wanted to ask me to marry him but I was disappointed the last time I thought he was going to ask me to marry him and he didn't and I didn't want to get my hopes up again.

Michael got the attention of every one. Then he said to his parents that he has finally found a lady that is wonderful, very nice, trust worthy, loving and that's just to mention a few. Then he turned to me and said baby these past ten months I have been so happy. Then he asked me do I love him I said very much. He then said that that is the answer he was looking for, that is all I need to know. He got down on one knee and asked me to marry him. You can just about think how happy and in shock I was. Then he gave me the most beautiful ring. I looked at Michael and said I would be happy to be your wife, yes I will marry you. Michael's father stood up and gave me a hug and then he shook Michael's hand and said son you have done well, Congratulations.

Michael's mother said Michael how can you marry someone you only knew ten months. Then she said you don't even know her. I just looked at Michael's father wondering what would make his wife act that way.

Mrs. Watts kept talking about Michael don't know me. Michael said I know her enough to know that I am going to marry her. Mr. Watts said that is enough. His mother decided to shut up finally. I was very uncomfortable being in their home after Michael's mother humiliated me.

When we were done eating, Michael and I went into the rooms they had prepared for us. Of course we had separate bedroom, I asked Michael could we go to a motel because I was uncomfortable being there? Michael asked me to just wait a little while. He was going to talk to his parents, I said ok.

I understood it when my friend Angel said that when she got a man worth being with that she hoped his parents are dead. She didn't wish for them to die. She wants them to be already dead and all their kids would be grown and live across the waters. I can get her point.

Michael told me to just focus on us getting married. He kissed me on my cheek. Then he went down stairs. I stayed in the bedroom. After about thirty minutes later Michael came back and said that everything was ok. Michael tried to make me feel better being in his parent's house, poor thing; I just faked it so he wouldn't be under to much stress.

Michael and I had a nice time despite his mother's rudeness. It was almost time for us to go home. Being on the cruise ship and going to Trinidad was two vacations in one. I was happy I didn't have to deal with his mother much because they lived far away.

It was beautiful. There were thousands of people on it. I loved it so much, I didn't want to go back home. It was so soothing, almost as if we were actually on land.

That was an experience that neither Michael nor I would ever forget. We made love almost the entire time on the ship. Our making it home time was quickly approaching.

When Michael and I made it home we were exhausted. The two of us were not in any shape to even talk. Michael stayed with me for a few days then he went to his big house a few miles away. I wonder why he had such a big house.

Chapter 28

Michael and I had been hard at work on planning our wedding. It was nice to be planning the wedding together. When I got married before I had to do everything and I mean everything on my own. The only thing he did was show up. You know I wished he would have not showed.

I have to give it to my ex-husband he was a good provider. I was happy most of the time, but to try and kill me that makes those nice things insignificant.

Anyway back to what's important. The wedding was beautiful. Michael's parents didn't show up, I wished his father would have come.

Michael and I were not able to go on a honeymoon after the wedding because he had to work, and he wanted our honeymoon to be a long one. His job needed for him to be there. Michael did tell me to just focus on where we were going to go for our honeymoon. Michael said I could plan to go anywhere I wanted to. Wow, I was so happy I almost shouted.

Michael was a wonderful man. He was also very romantic. He would always pull my chairs out for me and even open my side of the car door when we would go places. Just like at the beginning, but it was still nothing like my Dean. I know they were different but no one will ever be able to top my Dean. LORD help me!

Michael said he wanted to start working on having a baby right away. I really wanted us to have a few years together to enjoy each other, having a baby is a lot of work. Michael was adamant about having a baby so I said ok. We started on making a baby every time we got a chance.

By now we had been making love for months. One would think, after making love for so long, it had to be time for a pregnancy. Well unfortunately, a year had passed and I still wasn't pregnant. From there we went to the doctor to see if either one of us had a problem. We went and took a few tests, but we had to wait about a week for any kind of results. When the week was up, the doctor called us both in to have a consultation. As soon as we got there they called us straight into the office.

The doctor asked us to have a seat, and then Michael asked if there was a problem? The doctor said to him, "No, you're fine." Then he looked at me and said, Mrs. Watts, your test came back positive. "You have uterus cancer." I then asked him, "What about having a baby?" He told me I would never be able to have children. I looked at Michael, and saw the tears in his eyes. I asked the doctor what needed to be done about the cancer. He said he caught it really early, but I still had to have the surgery as soon as possible. This was my only choice if I didn't want it to spread and I wouldn't be able to do anything about it. He asked us if we needed any time alone to talk in his office, and we told him yes.

When the doctor left the room, Michael asked me in a serious tone," "we will never be able to have children?" The look on my face had to be terrifying. I started to think, should he be worried about my health? I said, "Michael, shouldn't you be worried about my health?" He said, the doctor said you'll be alright after the surgery, but you will not be able to give me a family." He made me feel as low as a dog. I was in disbelief about what he was saying.

The doctor came back into the room and asked us what our decision was. Then I asked how soon could it be done? The doctor asked the nurse to get me in as soon as possible. The nurse asked could I come in on Tuesday at seven o'clock in the morning. I asked Michael was that ok? He said yes so the nurse made the appointment.

When we got home it was total silence. The situation was so awkward because I was thinking about me having cancer and he was thinking about us not being able to have a family. Though he was very quiet, Michael did get up and take me to the hospital that Tuesday morning.

After we made it to the hospital, they had me to sign some papers. Then they wanted me to get into a hospital gown. I was very afraid. My husband was not even supporting me, I said to myself. I tried not to worry so much.

A nurse came in and started an IV. Then she put some medicine in it to calm my nerves. When the doctor came in he started asking me a lot of questions. Michael was sitting in a seat very far from me. The doctor asked me a question I didn't anticipate him asking, and it was when I had my last baby. I told him I never had one. He continued, saying there are signs showing that you've had at least one child. I had to tell the truth if it was important to my surgery.

I proceeded to tell the doctor that I was sorry I lied to him, but that part of my life I never wanted to conjure up ever again. I began by telling the doctor that I had had a baby when I was fifteen years old. My parents had gave my baby to a family to raise they said I was too young to take care of a baby. Michael looked at me like I was dirt. The look on his face gave me a chill throughout my body that I would never forget.

The nurse began to take me to the operating room. Michael still didn't say anything to me. He didn't know if I was going to wake up from the surgery or not. He just didn't seem to care one way or another. A feeling went through me that he would rather for me to come out the operating room dead.

After the three hours of surgery I was in the recovery room. After a few hours they put me in a regular room. There was no Michael in sight. I hated to think my husband didn't care about me at all.

I couldn't help but to think my past has come back to haunt me to the point that I wished that I would have never came through the surgery.

I was so lost in my life I didn't know what to do. When I was released from the hospital Michael had all my clothes packed and ready to send me on my way. I didn't know what to do. I called my friend Angel. Angel came to pick me up from sitting outside on the porch.

I didn't want to tell Angel about all the things I had been through. I just told her about not being able to have any children and that because I couldn't have any children Michael didn't want me anymore. I asked Angel would it be ok if I could stay with her until I was well enough to move around, she said yes. I knew she was going to say yes even if it was a inconvenience to her, which was the type of friend Angel was.

I told Angel I don't know how I was going to cope with my husband leaving me. Angel said I was going to be ok, she said for me to pray to the Lord that he would help me. Angel said it would not be easy but I will get through it. Angel said she would be right by my side as long as I needed her to be.

I was now well enough to leave Angel's house, she had been a good friend, but I needed to get going. I had no family, no husband, and no nothing. When I left Angel's house I didn't have any place to go. I promised to get even with Michael some day.

I knew this one girl that I had met over Angel's house a while back I started to hang with her so I would have some place to go. I moved out of my house to move in my husband's house. So I didn't have a place to stay. I was at the cross roads at this point in my life. I was not sure about what I was going to do with my life. I knew I wanted a big house with a tall fence and a big yard and a back and front porch, and someone to share that with. I was not looking for a man just yet. I had to get over this Michael stuff first. I knew this house thing was going to take a long time to get. I wanted a house but I didn't have any money. I didn't have a stable place to stay. I needed to make some money and in a hurry. So I became a call girl. If you ask me a call girl was still a fancy word for a whore with a little class.

I didn't like doing that at all but to get some fast money that's the quickest way I knew. After about three months I had saved enough money for a little apartment. I continued to whore myself for a few more months until I had saved enough money to pay up my rent for about six months then I quit. Being a fancy whore made me a lot of money but the work was hard. I guess you might want to know what was so hard about laying on my back, my front and my knees. Well it was extremely hard to have sex with a person just for money. It was not any fun being called sluts, bitches, and tramp was a few of their choice words I had to put up with, not to mention the black eyes and bruises. When I quit my call girl job I was stable for a while.

I was still in shock to know I was bought and sold after all those years. I finally knew why there were no twins or triplets. I still didn't know who I was. I went through a second bad marriage and the death of my Dean was breaking me down. It was almost unbearable to think of all the bad things that happened in my life. I couldn't take it any longer I wanted to just die.

Chapter 29

One day I was just sitting around with a thought to kill Michael. To stop those thoughts I decided to find something to do. I called my good friend Toni. I said to her there is something you and I need to talk about. Toni said she will be over in a little while.

I waited for Toni on pins and needles. I had to get into some kind of a project to keep me sane. After a few hours I heard a knock on the door. I said come in. It was Toni. I started to ask Toni what was going on. I knew that I was not a bad person. I had to think about my life. I figured out that the things that I had done in my lifetime I had to pay for all of it. I decided to take my punishment with a grain of salt and just live the best way I could. There was this one thing that was getting in my way, Michael. How do I stop the visions of Michael being dead? It is hard to put what he did to me in the back of my mind.

When Toni and I were talking I went on and told her that I cannot have any children. To my surprise Toni told me that she couldn't have any children either. Toni said she had a hysterectomy. I told her I had also had one because I had uterus cancer and I didn't get proper medical care when I had that baby when I was fifteen. Toni said that she had to have a hysterectomy because of a enlarge uterus.

Toni said our life was messed up. I said to Toni I don't think I can take all of these bad things that had gone wrong in my life. Toni said we don't have a choice or to just die. I was not ready to die before I kill Michael. I will just deal with this mess in my life the best way I knew how. I then said you know Toni, it went through my mind that what goes around comes around. No ifs ands or buts about it.

Toni began to say that our past has caught up with us. I asked Toni what she was talking about. Toni said that since we are not able to have children of our own that maybe we should get a business going and make our past work for us. I asked Toni what kind of business she was talking about. Toni said that she was doing what our parents had done, selling babies. I was surprised that Toni would say something like that. The past has been a nightmare to me and Toni. I didn't need a reminder about that. I asked Toni was she sure that she wanted to do this? Toni said yes. I told Toni I needed a little time to think about that.

I had been contemplating what I was going to do. I gave it a lot of thought. I called Toni to tell her that I was in with her. My life was already painful, adding a little excitement and making money at the same time wouldn't have bothered me at all. I needed to make a living somehow so I can get started on my dream house.

Toni had already had a few customers lined up. I asked Toni how long had she been thinking about this? She said that she had been thinking about it since her marriage ended, and that she had already sold two babies.

I was still fighting with my husband doing me the way he did. He made me feel less of a woman leaving me, because I was unable to give him any children. This brought back memories of my first marriage. Both of my husband's had sent my self-esteem at an all time low. I knew I needed to put that behind me but it was very hard. Working with Toni would take up a lot of my time. I would have the business to focus on. That would keep me out of trouble.

I called Toni, she wanted us to get together to talk about the business. She invited me to dinner. She had cooked a big dinner for us. She was in the same boat I was in, not having any children, no man or any family at all.

We had a nice dinner while talking about the business. She seemed to have everything in control. She already had some clients and some pregnant girls lined up to make some quick cash roll in. She had this pregnant teenager that wanted to give up her baby. She even has a couple that wanted two babies. The girl that was going to give her baby up name was Shaun. Shaun said she had a few friends that didn't want their babies because they were too young to take care of any children.

I asked Toni how the babies were going to be delivered, she said that they go to the hospital to have the baby, then she would make sure when they are released they went to Toni's house. Then they gave the babies to Toni because their parents didn't want to take care of any babies, so most of their parents was OK with it. Sometimes the parents would bring their daughters over to the house.

I told Toni I was a little worried that we might get caught, like our parents did. Toni said this was a better set up than what her parents had. I thought about me being the one to get our parents locked up in prison. I didn't want to go to prison. Toni said that she didn't have to recruit any pregnant girls that they came to her already willing to give their babies up. She said these girls tell their friends that they were pregnant and couldn't let their parents know. Some of those girls didn't even show a lot even at nine months. They were anxious to give their babies away for one reason or another.

We needed to be careful not to have any records in a place no one knows where they were. We wouldn't have a delivery room. There are no men around to be sleeping with the girls. We just need to be more cautious. We even had some adult women that didn't want to keep their babies that would come to us for help.

I've been talking to women that I knew couldn't conceive any babies that was eager to get a baby the quickest way they knew how. I already had five customers waiting on a baby.

The girls just come over to visit. We couldn't let a lot of teenage girls be at the house that would draw more attention to us. I had them call me when they needed help. Toni asked me what I thought. I told her it sounded good to me.

Chapter 30

I moved in with Toni. I didn't want to be alone. It was going to be tough knowing the reason my husband left me. I knew I had to find a reason to get even with Michael. I would not be at peace until he was dead at least close to death. It dawned on me that my husband abandon me and that he was rich and I could get a lot of money from him but I was so focus on him being dead that getting money out of him was not relevant. That's how much I had been hurt that I didn't care about the money. I was in need of a therapist, "bad".

When I got all my things and moved in with Toni she and I had talked all day about our problems. We both had become very angry. I had to focus on the business at hand. Toni had a nice set up. These girls didn't have a clue their babies were being sold. They thought they were given to families that didn't have children.

I was all for making money but I had mostly killing my husband who left me in the hospital not knowing if I came out alive or dead. I couldn't let that go, Michael will pay, and he will die! Going through depression, Post Traumatic Stress Syndrome, mental and physical abuse anxiety and panic attacks and a lot of other terrible things, I was on the verge of snapping. I focus more on getting even than anything else.

Toni showed me the paper work on the girls that are waiting to have their babies. And she showed me the names of some of her customers. I was not a person who cares for paper work.

Paper work would get you prison time or dead. I told Toni I didn't want any paper work around. She reassured me that the paper work she had was only sticky notes that are torn up as soon as we are done with them. Toni said she had another copy hidden in a good spot in the house.

Toni never knew I was the one that gave the authorities the evidence that put our families in prison and I plan to never let her find out. This time it's a lot different than when our parents had the business. They had too much evidence around that would get them in trouble they couldn't get out of.

We won't have any men around to cause any problems. Toni and I both agreed to that. Most men are trouble in one way or another but they were necessary.

The girls that were already pregnant came to us as a last resort. We got a lot of business because the girls knew other girls that parents were upset about them being pregnant that they were willing to go along with them giving up their babies. That was how we would get some of the business.

We were selling the babies for no less than ten thousand dollars. We would do research on potential customers, that is how we find out if they had a lot of money or not. We focus our attention to the houses they lived in and what neighborhood they lived in and the cars they drove to base the amount we were asking to get paid for the babies. I had remembered some of the family business from when I was a teenager.

Chapter 31

The business at hand for me to tend to is that so called man that I was married too. He would never have a chance to do to another woman what he did to me.

I knew what time Michael went to work and what time he got off. I had not yet figured out what I would do to take him down. I went to his house to case out the place to make sure there wasn't anything different going on around there.

I had to go to the house because one of the girls was in labor. She still had a ways to go, but this baby was ready to come into the world. Her pain was about thirty minutes apart. When they are about ten minutes apart we take them to the hospital. I didn't go to the hospital with her. Toni went but she only dropped her off at the emergency department. We didn't want to get too involved in being seen with the girls too often.

Shaun was to call us when she had the baby and when she was to be released.

In the meantime I focused on Mr. Michael. I went to his job to see if I could spot his car. It was in the parking lot. I still had not decided what I was going to do to get even with him. But I knew it would have to be a perfectly planned out execution. I had been stalking him every day now. I wanted to get him in a way that he was looking at me eye to eye.

Toni called the hospital to see if Shaun had her baby. The hospital wouldn't give her any information on the phone; we had to wait until Shaun called us.

I had finally thought I had met the man of my dreams. Michael treated me like a princess up until I became no use to him. My dream became the worst nightmare ever. I guess I can't figure out which marriage was the worst. If I had to bet on it would have been the first marriage.

Michael was almost as heartless as James, but not quite. I thought my life was beginning to be worth living. I was let down because I put too much into a man instead of putting the Lord at the head of our relationship.

I tried to change my mind about trying to pay him back. But the devil kept telling me to do something to Michael. I love my Lord and I knew it was wrong to think of doing bad things. That's why my life had been so bad. Almost all my life I had so many setbacks I never thought that I would accomplish anything. Something had to change.

The phone rang. It was Shaun; she said she had had a baby boy. She would be released from the hospital the next day Toni would go and pick her up. Toni and I already had a buyer. The couple that was buying the baby is well off financially.

Toni had gone to pick up Shaun from the hospital. When they returned home Toni already had a few things for the baby.

Shaun's baby went to this couple that owned their own Realty Company. They were loaded with money. They were unable to have children of their own. They were waiting to buy another baby later on. Their names are Mr. and Mrs. Reed. They said after nine months they wanted to buy a little girl. They wanted to raise them as their own and if they were the same age's people would know something was wrong.

I drove by Michael's house last night. I saw him pulling up in the yard with a woman. Much as I hated Michael a part of me was hurting when I saw him with another woman. Now I wanted to kill him, but I was too hurt, I would have gotten caught if I was to do something in a murderous rage. I had to get away from them fast.

When I returned home I didn't want to talk to anyone not even Toni. I was crying so hard I could have drowned in my own tears. I just wanted to be alone.

I was unable to sleep the whole night long. I just kept seeing him with the other woman in what use to be our home. Just the thought and vision was enough for me to go over there with two guns and empty them both into his bodies. I was thinking that Michael was making love to her the way he made love to me. I better stop thinking so hard. I want to go over there and turn matrix on them. I will take a sleeping pill to put me to sleep fast before I become front page news.

It was morning now I told Toni what had happened to me the night before. I didn't want to talk to anyone. Toni gave me some news I just couldn't live with. Toni said she heard that this female and my husband were going to have a baby together. When I heard that I was over powered with rage I had never experienced before. I got up from the table and went to my room and loaded my guns. The vision I had was about to become reality. Toni ran behind me and shook me back into reality.

I was planning the murder. I had to figure it out if the woman was going to hell with him or not. Toni needed me to help her with the business.

Another girl was in labor. Her pains were about five minutes apart. Toni asked me to take Shay, that's the girls name to the hospital. Toni also wanted me to open up an account. Toni said it wouldn't look right for that much money to be in her account. So after taking shay to the hospital I went to the bank to open up and account. Toni gave me ten thousand dollars to open the account with. So I took care of that.

When I made it back to the house Toni said Shay had a baby boy. She said both of them were doing well and would be getting out of the hospital tomorrow. So I calmed myself down and focused on making all this money.

Toni said she was being paid ten thousand dollars for this baby. I had to pick Shay up from the hospital. Toni said the lady that was going to buy this baby was single and didn't have a lot of money and that's why she only charged her the small amount of ten thousand dollars.

It was three in the afternoon when the baby was picked up. When Toni got the money she gave it to me to put in my account.

Chapter 32

It was time to get back to Michael. I am executing a plan to get even with him. I still had a key to the back door of our home we once shared. I waited for him to go to work. I made sure that that woman's car was gone before I went in. To my surprise the key still worked, that was dumb of him, and good for me. When I went in, to my surprise again Michael had changed everything around and had bought new everything, but the fool didn't change the lock, go figure. He had gotten a king size bed. He had new living room and dining room furniture. Michael had changed everything. I was becoming more and more enraged. That just gave me more guts to take him out, as if I needed more convincing. I was so overwhelmed by all of these changes. Michael had not too long gotten new furniture. That just led me to think that he was just trying to get any existing of me ever being in his house out. I decided not to do anything because I was to upset. I didn't want to make a mistake and get caught from being to mad. When I left Michael's house I was so upset that I could barely drive home.

When I got home Toni was sitting in the living room watching TV. I must have had a peculiar expression on my face. I told Toni what I was going to do. She said maybe I shouldn't do it. I was not hearing what she was saying. I wanted him dead and as soon as possible. I told Toni that I was going to go to my room to cool off.

A few days later I went back to Michael's house. When I was looking around the house I found a love note from Michael to Shirley. It said to a wonderful lady that had been my dream lady. You had made me a different man. I wanted a woman that can get love and give love unconditionally. I have been looking for a woman like you for a long time. I have never been in love like this before, but after meeting you I could say you are the woman for me. I love you very much. Thanks for being the best woman a man could ever have, from your man, Michael. Can you believe this crap? I wished I could kill him a thousand times.

I brought with me some gray tape, the tape of all tape. This was going to be a celebration. I had both of my guns loaded. Michael was gone long enough for me to fix him dinner. I cooked all of his favorite foods. He liked T-bone steak, baked sweet potatoes and broccoli. For dessert I baked a peach cobbler. I was already to do this.

It was time for him to be getting home. I had parked my car a few blocks away so he wouldn't have a clue that I was there. When I heard Michael coming I hid in the closet. I heard him calling for Shirley. Then he made a statement like I can smell my favorite foods. That statement meant Michael had given Shirley a key to the house. It is going to be even easier to do him in. I jumped from the closet with my two guns and said, "honey I'm home".

Michael's eyes became glazed like to big glazed donuts. He said Lagretto why are you in my house with guns pointed at me. I said well I decided a while back that I was going to kill you. I said to Michael; forgive me for taking a long time.

Michael was so nervous he was tripping over his words. He said Lagretto please leave my house. I said husband this suppose to be our home. I said to Michael what's wrong boo; I'm used to you being so vociferous? But now the cat got your tongue.

I asked Michael was he hungry. I told him I had cooked his favorite foods, he said thank you. I said anytime while you are alive.

Michael said he was sorry for whatever He had did to me and please forgive him. Michael, I said you don't know what you did to me? I then said, so Shirley is the best thing that has ever happened to you? I read the letter you wrote to her. What kind of woman am I? He said you are a good woman. Then he said I don't know what was wrong with me. Then he apologized to me for the tenth time. I was growing old listening to Michael. I pulled out my rope and the old dependable gray tape; y'all know what kind of tape I was talking about. I had Michael to sit at the kitchen table so I could rope and tape him to the chair. Then I sat across from him. I said to Michael I want you to tell me again what kind of woman I am? He began by trying to tell me he was devastated by us not being able to have children. I looked Michael in the eyes and said I am tired of men. Y'all don't have any respect for yourselves or anyone else. When it happens to you I wish I could be there to slap your face if you even blink wrong. I forgot you won't be here. Men can be so cruel and hurtful. Why can't men have a heart like a woman and just be a little sensitive when they fall out of love. I forgot again those women at my ex-husband's job don't mind if their husbands cheat because they didn't care about my husband cheating. That is one place I would love to be when one of their husbands cheat on them. For what they said about me I know they will be quiet as a church mouse because it was OK when my husband did it to me.

Why do men have to leave a woman so scared and shameful, hurtful and with low–self-esteem and feeling like they are so low that you can look at a snake eye to eye. Most men are not even worth even having a good woman, only for just a necessity. Otherwise men can be junked like an old car. Out of women and men look at all the men you have known in your lifetime and tell me how many were any good. I don't mean slightly well, I mean just a good man that will just make simple mistakes a woman can deal with without losing herself in the process. I have heard women say that they would rather have any kind of man as long as they have one. That's so sad. Men act like they are superior to women like the white people used to and some still think they are. These men, not all will treat another race better than they own race, especially you ball players. A black woman put up with your bad habits, bad breath, cheating, not taking care of your family beating on us mentally and physically. It really kills me that when black men get some good money they find them a white woman to share that with. Then when things are said about it they want to put it on a sister that she is not doing what she is supposed to do whatever that means. They start to say that we are mean or whatever. What are the reasons we are mean, maybe because you are lazy won't take out the trash, cheating, disrespectful and don't take care of the home financially on top a lot of other things. Some of us women need to check ourselves also.

The only man that I had that was about something was dead. Why do the good die young? Why can't some of these devils like you Michael die young like a dog? I hate the type of men like my ex-husband. And now you are going to pay for what you have done to me and for other women you have done the way you did me. And you are even going to pay for what men in the future are going to do to me. Michael you have made me almost lose my mind.

I had forgotten for a minute that Shirley had a key to the house. I had put the chain on the door so she would have to knock to get in.

After a few minutes Shirley was knocking on the door for Michael to open because it had the chain on it. I went to open it to let her in. I made her sit in another chair at the kitchen table. I made Shirley eat dinner with us after I had micro waved it because it had gotten cold. I fed the both of them because they were roped and duct taped. Shirley asked who was I and what did I want? I told her I was only Michael's wife. Shirley had a strange look on her face. After I made sure everything was secure I went home to check on everything. Toni was cooking lunch for everyone. Toni acts like she is bipolar. Sometimes she can just be so sweet and then with the blink of an eye she can be the devil.

Toni said she had to run an errand and that she will be back soon. I needed to go to Michael and Shirley's place. I told the girls

I had something to do and I would be back in a few hours. I went to Michael's house. When I got close I parked a few blocks away and walked to the house. I planned to kill him before the neighbors get suspicious.

I said to Michael are you ready to die? I took the towel off his mouth so he could answer my question. Michael started to beg for me not to kill him. I said with a soft voice baby I am not sorry and I'm going to kill you.

The only thing left to do was come up with the way I was going to do it. I knew I couldn't shoot him because it would be too noisy. I guess I would just use a knife. I told Michael that I was going to be creative in killing him, as for you Shirley I would give you a break because you didn't have a thing to do with this, or did you?

I put a pot of water on the stove. I let the water boil until it started to evaporate. I said to Michael do you want to know what I am going to do to you. He said no. I said I will tell you anyway. I told Michael I wanted to see him take his last breath. I told him I was going to re-circumcise him. I let him know that I had not planned how I was going to kill him, that I was just doing it as I go.

The first thing I did was to untie Michael from the kitchen table. I had my guns to his head then I had him to go into the bedroom and lay down on his new king size bed that he bought for him and Shirley.

Michael was still begging me not to kill him. I asked what about your woman? Michael just kept begging until I put the towel back in his mouth. I told him I was getting tired of him whining like a baby.

After I got the both of them situated. I wanted Shirley to watch me kill Michael. I quickly changed that, I wanted Michael to watch me kill Shirley. Since you both are so in love you can be together in death, isn't that nice? I shouted isn't that nice, I slapped Michael and told him to answer me, even with the towel in his mouth. Of course he couldn't answer me he could only nod his head.

I told Shirley it's time for her to die, and then I just nicely sliced her throat. I then said to Michael I know you wish you could die like your woman. Well husband I am not sorry that your death will not be so easy.

I took Michael's towel from his mouth so I could get a last conversation. I said to Michael now it's unfortunate that you and Shirley will not be having y'all little bundle of joy.

I said to Michael since we couldn't have any children together you were not going to have any with no one else. Michael said what are you talking about? I said Michael when was Shirley's due date? Michael said did you think she was pregnant? I said wasn't she? Michael said no. I said oops! My bad that were the only reason she died. There's nothing I can do about that now.

Anyway getting back to you player. Michael quickly said please don't kill me; I will do anything you ask. I said to Michael I am not sorry. Besides I cannot break a promised I made to you about killing you, that's not right is it? I promise you that I was going to kill you so I have to do just that. If I would not have promised I would kill you I may have changed my mind, I am sorry, "not." I have to keep my word; you know your word is your bond. You don't want anyone calling me a liar do you? Of course not, I said.

I went to the kitchen to get the hot water to take to the bedroom. I looked Michael in the eyes and said, very soon my husband. I cut Michaels clothes off him. I got the hot water and proceeded to pour it all over Michael. The look on his face was terrifying. I then took my knife and made lots of small cuts all over his body. Then I rubbed salt and pepper in his cuts that still didn't seem to satisfy me. No I had to be even more drastic and creative. I then used my knife to re-circumcise him. After a few hours I became bored so I just went ahead and slit his throat to put him out of his misery. Wasn't that nice of me? I had to finish him, because I was becoming bored.

After I was done enjoying myself I set the house on fire then I went home. I buried the guns and the knives in Toni's back yard. Then I went to my room and took off the incriminating evidence I had on and took a shower.

I was tired from killing Michael that I just went to bed. After sleeping a few hours Toni woke me up. Toni began to tell me there was a breaking news report that a house on Dyson Street was set on fire and as the firemen put out the fire they discovered two bodies in the house tied up with rope and duck tape. Toni said they couldn't release any details until they notify the next of kin. Toni said Lagretto the house looked like Michael's. At that moment I could have dropped dead. It sounded like the bodies didn't burn up.

If they didn't burn that meant they were able to gather up evidence. Why didn't I make sure they had burned? Now I may be in a lot of hot water myself if they found evidence on me.

Toni asked me did I go through with killing Michael. I said yes. I said I poured hot water on him and then I made lots of small cuts on him and then I rubbed pepper and salt in the wombs, then I re-circumcised him then I just slit his throat I told Toni that I hid the knife and guns in her back yard. Toni gave me a look as if I was the devil himself. I began to wonder about that myself. See what a man would do to you? The look she gave me sent chills all over my body. Then she went to the kitchen to cook dinner.

Chapter 33

As I was sitting around all of a sudden I started to feel strange. There was a warm feeling going through my chest. Then my head started to feel weird. I knew then I was having an anxiety attack. I believed with all my heart that my wrong doings was coming back to haunt me. I began to panic. I was calling on JESUS. I needed him to help me. I felt like I was going crazy. Having a panic attack would have you calling on anyone but Satan.

I was praying to my LORD then I asked myself why the LORD will do anything for me as much sinning I had done and still doing.

This panic attack was too much for me. I asked Toni to get me to the hospital fast. I was rocking back and forward shaking very bad. It seems like every time I do something wrong some kind of disaster happens to me. What goes around comes around, and boy does it ever.

When we got to the hospital it seemed as if they were taking their own sweet time to call my name. I couldn't sit still at all. The nurse finally called my name. After the nurse came in the room she took some blood to see if something was going on besides a panic attack. I was so impatient waiting on the lab work so they can give me something to calm me down.

Finally the doctor told the nurse to give me some Ativan. The nurse was taking her time again. When the nurse came in my room to give me my Ativan I was very happy. The medicine calmed me down. After they released me I immediately looked in the phone book for a new Medical doctor. I needed to see a doctor so I can have some medication on hand at all times.

After I found a doctor I told him that I had started to have anxiety and panic attacks often again. The doctor ordered some blood work to see if I had been on drugs. I had always had a lot of back pain. Without me having a doctor I had to do what I had to do and that was to go to the hospital all the time or buy some pain pills off the streets, so I most of the time chose to buy some from someone I knew that had some.

When the blood work came back positive for morphine I was puzzled. I was not taking any morphine. I know I did take a pain pill from one of my friends. I would have never guessed it had any morphine in it. I thought it was just a vicodin. Of course my doctor didn't believe me. From that moment on that Dr. had me labored as a drug addict. I know when I was a drug addict and it wasn't then.

That doctor treated me different every time I went to see him. This doctor diagnosed me with Fibro Myalgia, a disease that causes a lot of pain. Imagine a doctor diagnosing you with a painful illness and not giving you anything to help with the pain. Then he wanted to know why I was getting medication off the streets. I said because you want prescribe me any pain medicine. If I had my own I wouldn't have to get other peoples medicine.

Each time I went to see him he would talk about me being a drug addict. I had since giving up street drugs that he didn't know anything about. I knew if I would have told him about my past what would he have said then? He was already making me feel like I was on drugs just a different type that I had been on. Each time I went to see him he made me feel like a junky. One other time I went to see him he had the nerve to ask me to hold out my hand to see if I was shaking then he told me I was having drug withdrawals when

I was actually having a hot flash like I do all day long any way. I just happen to be having one in front of him. I was not having drug withdrawal. Little did he know I had some pain medicine in my purse. I was not just out to get high, I was in pain. If he was not going to prescribe me any for the pain I was going through I had to do something to stop the pain. He didn't prescribe me any so I went to my car and took those I had in my purse. I really didn't want to take any one else's medicine but what was I to do?

I went to see him again about the pain in my back he said it was my Fibro Myalgia. I had become afraid of this doctor because there could be something else going on with my body and he would put it all on my Fibro Myalgia. The last time I walked in his office he wanted to talk about me being an addict at that moment I walked out his door never to return again. Don't let your doctor tell you that everything that hurts you is your Fibro Myalgia because it can be something else hurting you and you will be diagnosed wrong and that it could be a matter of life or death.

Chapter 34

It has been a while since I killed Michael and Shirley. No policeman had come to the house yet. I was so nervous about the police that I couldn't rest. I was looking out the window all day and night. I would shake so bad when I would hear a car pulling up in the yard. I was even nervous when I heard the phone ring. It was especially hard to sleep, not because I had killed Michael and Shirley but because I might get caught.

Toni had started to become hostile towards me. I tried to stay out of her way. The only time we talked was when we were discussing business.

One of the girls went into labor. I took her to the hospital. This time I went into the hospital because Karen was afraid to be by herself. The nurse asked me to fill out the paper work because Karen was in so much pain. I didn't know much about Karen so I went over to her so she could tell me the information about her. After I was done with the paper work I told Karen I had to go. I told her to call me after she had the baby.

When I got back to the house Toni was giving me strange looks. I thought she was just going through something.

The phone was ringing I was afraid to answer it. Toni answered it. It was for her.

When Toni got off the phone she told me to call a lady that wanted to buy a baby boy. Toni said let her know that Karen is in labor now. She wanted me to let the lady know to be prepared for the baby.

I began to notice that Toni was beginning to talk to me like I was her employee instead of her partner. I knew I came in late and Toni had her business going already. But when I started to go into business with her she lead me to believe I was her partner, not just an employee of hers.

So a little time passed by and Toni was still acting strange. Something told me that it was time to move on. I think I needed to talk to her about the way she had been treating me lately. But I will wait until Karen has her baby and when we sell it before I say anything.

Karen called to say she had a baby girl. Toni was so upset. I asked her what was wrong. She said Mrs. Charles wanted a baby boy. Toni said for me to call Mrs. Charles and try to talk her into taking the baby girl in place of the baby boy. So I did. When I got Mrs. Charles on the phone she was upset about the baby being a girl. I tried my best in trying to talk her into taking the baby girl. She said "no" her husband wanted to have a boy he could call his own. She said to call her back when we got a boy, I said OK. Then I hung up the phone and told Toni what Mrs. Charles said.

Toni was so upset she said to me why couldn't I talk Mrs. Charles into taking the girl? I told her Mrs. Charles was not hearing that about a baby girl. I also told her Mrs. Charles said her husband wanted a baby boy he could call his Jr.

Toni said she should have called herself. She said to me that I couldn't do anything right. I asked her what her problem was. Toni was upset so I went to my room before I lost my temper and had to find another place to stay. So I chose not to cut off my nose to spite my face. So I kept my distance.

It was time for one of us to pick up Karen. I wanted to go pass Michael's house so I said to Toni, I would go and pick Karen up for

164

her. As I was driving down the street I became so nervous when I looked up the street and saw the yellow crime tape around Michael's house. There was this man looking around the house. I was almost too nervous to drive from shaking so bad. I made sure I was at a safe distant from Michael's house so no one would notice me. A little time had gone past, so I didn't understand why someone was still going over to "our" house. It was time for them to be tearing it down by now or remodeling it. I guess I should have been claiming what was mine. I just wanted to know what the outcome of my life was going to be before I claim anything.

I finally got to the hospital. I picked up Karen and the baby. Then I headed home. When I got to the house I asked Toni could I talk to her for a minute, she said yes. I asked her have she heard anything about Michael? Toni said she saw the news. I asked her what they said. She said they were talking about Michael and Shirley being murdered. Then she said the news said that the way Michael was killed was so gruesome that it was like someone was enraged with hate. I looked at Toni; she had a look on her face that made me feel like I was a demon. At that moment I felt like I was a monster. Toni had looked at me like that a lot lately.

It had been a few weeks since I killed Michael and Shirley. I still hadn't heard from the police. I didn't understand why they were taking so long to come and question me.

Toni had been acting better towards me. I asked her did she have a buyer for the baby girl. She said yes and that they would be coming to pick her up that day. I asked Toni how much was she getting paid for the baby. Toni said fifteen thousand dollars I asked Toni how much she was going to pay me. She said five thousand dollars; I wanted to see if the amount I found on a post-it matched. I couldn't believe Toni would try and get over on me. The post-it said she was getting paid twenty five thousand dollars for that baby. I said to myself what was really going on?

A few hours later a lady came to the house. I had never seen her before. Toni wanted to talk to her alone so they went into the office to talk privately. When Toni was done talking to the lady they came out the office. I went into the living room to get the baby and I gave her to the lady.

After they were gone Toni called me into the office and gave me my money. I had been getting paid half the amount that was paid to Toni. When Toni gave me the money I said thank you. I didn't say too much to her because I needed a place to stay. I didn't need any problems at that moment.

Today was a quiet and pleasant beautiful day. I woke up feeling good. I was ready to face what life would bring. Toni had cooked a nice breakfast. It was nothing fancy just bacon and grits. When we were finished eating one of the girls had to be taken to the hospital. Toni and I both took her to the hospital. She was almost ready to have the baby any minute.

We made it to the hospital just in time, but it was a close call. The baby was born ten minutes after we got her there. She had a seven pound baby boy. We were very happy. We could breathe again.

Toni called Mrs. Charles so she could come and pick the baby up. Toni said the Charles' had their baby boy. Mrs. Charles was very happy. I was happy it was over trying to give them their boy.

After all this with Mrs. Charles it finally dawned on me that I had met her at church a little while back. That brought back some memories that I didn't care to relive.

This morning when I woke up Toni was up and packed and ready to go on a trip I knew nothing about. Toni said she would be gone a few days. I didn't ask her where she was going because I didn't care. Toni asked me would I take care of everything. It was very short notice but I said OK. So Toni was on her way to her mysterious journey.

Toni left a note telling me the prices the babies are to be sold for if one of the girls had their baby before she got back home.

Toni was going to be so upset when she got home. One of the girls that were going to have their baby changed her mind. I guess she just simply changed her mind, it happens sometimes.

It was time for Toni to return home. I didn't care about Toni taking a little trip but I had started to wonder where she went to. I don't know why Toni just up and went to some place that she wouldn't tell me where. Toni was beginning to seem like she was a stranger to me. She was always angry with me. I was wondering if she knew that I was the one that set up her parents. I didn't know but I was tired of walking on egg shells around her. If she had a problem with me she could work it out on her own. I was not about to go through any mess with her.

Toni had made it home. She had already had an attitude when she walked in the house. I hoped I didn't have to kick her butt, or she kicked mine when I told her about one of the girl's being gone. Toni was looking around the house. I guess she was looking for the girls. I then told her that one of the girls's left. She asked me what I meant. I said she changed her mind. Toni then had the audacity to ask me what I did to her. I told her she just simply changed her mind like I just told you. Toni was swearing and calling me any and everything. She finally got quiet and went in her room when I told her she better leave me the hell alone.

The next day Toni got up and cooked us breakfast. I was surprised to see she had cooked for the both of us. When I sat down to eat, Toni apologized to me for being so mean. I accepted her apology. That took the weight off my shoulders. It was hard to work around someone that had their nose up in the air.

We only had one girl. Business was slow. We just hung around the house waiting and hoping some business would come along soon. I needed more money to venture out on my own.

As Toni and I were sitting around not doing anything there was a knock on the front door. It was strange because everyone that knew us would go to the back. When I got up and answered the door I could have died at that moment when they respond was "this is the police!" They said they were looking for Lagretto Watts. I couldn't say anything different because by now they had to have a picture of me. I said I was Lagretto Watts. The officer said he needed to ask me some questions. He said they had been trying to reach me for quite some time. The officers asked, when was the last time I saw Michael? I said maybe two months ago. He then said, also by now I should know my husband was murdered. I said yes I did, I had seen the news. Then he began to ask me questions I was not prepared for. He asked why I was not at his funeral. I said because I didn't find out until it was all over. Then he asked why haven't I been in contact with the family? I told him that I was not close to my in-laws. Then he asked a question that almost blew me away. The officer said why I haven't come forward to claim my insurance. I had for some reason forgotten about the insurance policy. Michael said that he had taken my name off the policy. I didn't have any reason to believe Michael would lie about it. I told the officer I had forgotten about the insurance policy. I did tell the officer that I guess I didn't think much about it because Michael told me that he had taken my name off it.

The officer asked how Michael and I ended up apart. I said Michael and I were at odds with each other. Then he asked me why was that was? I didn't want to relive what I had been through with Michael. I wanted to forget that nightmare. I had to buy a minute or two before I answered that question.

I told the officer about the reason that Michael and I were separated. The officer then asked where I was on the seventeenth of September. I told the officer that I didn't remember where I was on that day. I looked at Toni and asked her did she recall where I was on that day? Toni said she didn't remember either where I was.

I knew I had to be in big trouble without an alibi. The officer said for me not to leave town because they would need to question me in detail at a later date. I told the officer that I had no reason to leave.

I was so nervous from then on. I had to check on the Insurance. A few days later I went to the Insurance Company. When I got there I found out that I was still the beneficiary. It was for Two hundred and fifty thousand dollars. I was even more nervous about the amount of the insurance because that was a good reason to make me the prime suspect alone with me not having an alibi. I told Toni about the insurance policy.

Toni said they had enough to focus on me being the prime and only suspect. I asked Toni what I should do. She said that there was nothing I could do but wait. I tried to push everything in the back of my mind. It was not easy at all.

Toni had gotten us some more business. Toni said for me to be careful because the police might come back over. It had been a while since the police had came over. The business was booming. I asked Toni maybe we should lay low. Toni said that it would be OK and just to be more cautious.

A girl named Claudia had come over. She was about fifteen years old and eight months pregnant. Toni asked Claudia did she have any friends that were pregnant. Claudia said she had two friends that were.   She also said that they were only a few months. Claudia said that she only knew where one of them lived. She said she knew them from school.

Toni asked Claudia could she tell her friends about what they could do if they didn't want their babies. Toni said to Claudia that there were no grownups that knew about what we were doing. She asked her not to tell them because we would not be able to help you girls if anyone found out. Toni also told Claudia that if they found out that the people that can't have babies would not be able to adopt one from us if any grownups find out. Toni said that people don't understand what we are trying to do. Then she said to Claudia, "wouldn't you like to be able to help someone to be able to care for and love the baby that you are not able to keep?" I remember someone giving me that same speech some years back.

Chapter 35

I got the strangest phone call that surprised me. It was Michael's mother's lawyer. He's calling me to see if I wanted to settle on a case against me on behalf of Michael Watt's parents. The lawyer said I was being sued by Michael's parents for the cost of Michael's funeral? It dawned on me that I was still legally married to Michael, well that I was Michael's widow. Being married made me responsible for all financial obligations. I didn't want anything to do with Michael when he was alive let alone with him being dead.

Michael's parents had paid for the funeral because I was nowhere to be found. I was somewhere to be found alright, they just didn't know where. If I would have been there I would have had Michael cremated like I almost did before.

I myself would not have spent that much money on him being dead.   To get this past me and to be left alone I told the lawyer that I would settle to pay them five thousand dollars. They were asking for six thousand dollars. They took the five thousand dollars. I didn't have to worry about that anymore.

Now that Michael no longer existed I had to work on getting the insurance money. The insurance agent said that because there was evidence of a homicide that they couldn't release any money until I was ruled out as a suspect or a year whichever one comes first. The agent then said that he was sorry. That was just what I didn't want to hear was "I am sorry."

I had to be cool, calm and focused on the business at hand. I had to do all the transaction in the business because I was just an employee. So I had to get back to work.

I was told to make the phone calls to the potential customers. Toni had three clients lined up. They all wanted a baby boy as soon as possible. That was going to take some time for three boys, unless we get lucky. We only had one girl that was going to deliver any day now. Toni told me to make an appointment to take this girl to have an ultrasound to see what she was having. I could only get an appointment two weeks from then. Susan was very close to having her baby. I didn't understand why Toni couldn't wait for Susan to deliver. Susan just happens to have gone into labor the day before the ultrasound was to be taken. Toni said I needed to take Susan to the hospital. So I did what my boss told me to do.

This baby was coming fast. Susan almost had the baby in the car at the front of the emergency department. I had to put the car in park and shout for some help. A few minutes later Susan had a beautiful baby girl. I said to myself that Toni was going to be mad. After I had found out that she was OK I headed for home. I told Toni that she had a girl. Toni's responds was damn, damn, damn. Then she said maybe I can call one of the clients to see if I can talk one of them into taking a beautiful baby girl.

It was a few months since the police had been to the house. There was a knock on the door when I went to see who was at the door I nearly passed out. It was the police again. I had just enough strength to ask the officer may I help him. To my surprise they wanted Toni to ask her some questions. Toni was not home when the officer was looking for her. The officer gave me a card to give Toni so she can give him a call when she gets in.

When Toni got home I gave her the card and told her that the officer wanted her to call him so he can ask her some questions about Michael's death. Toni said she don't want to be involved with any of this business. She then made a statement that she was not a killer. That statement made me feel like I was Satan. I was hurt by what Toni said. In reality she told the truth, I was a killer.

I asked Toni what she was going to say. Toni said she didn't see anyone kill anybody that made me feel a little better.

I was sitting down watching TV when I started to feel very bad. I had to be taken to the hospital. When I got there they took some blood work to see if they could find out what was wrong with me.

The blood work came out normal. I knew something was seriously wrong with me. They didn't find anything in my blood to indicate I was sick. The doctor asked me did I notice anything going on with my body that was different with my body lately. I said the only thing I could think of was I had a sore spot in my throat. So she ordered a test that I had to be at the hospital three times in the same day. They found out I had and over active thyroid, they admitted me in the hospital. The doctor said it was from not having sufficient enough iodine in our drinking water that could have caused my thyroid to not work properly or at all. Well mine didn't work at all. I was there for two week, staying in the hospital that long was making me lose out on thousands of dollars. There was nothing that I could do. By the time I got out the hospital Toni had sold four babies.

I was missing all kinds of money. The insurance was on hold. I really needed to make some more money, so I could get a place of my own.

I had saved about twenty thousand dollars of my own. I noticed Toni wasn't asking me to put money away in my account anymore. She even asked me what I put in my account that was hers to take it out. I guess she was nervous since the police was on my heels so tough.

After the police questioned Toni I had not heard anything else from them. Two months had passed with no words from the police. I was still their prime suspect.

When I got out of the hospital it was business as usual. Toni had me do all the transactions, "while she was being the boss."

172

I found a piece of paper with the name Wallace on it with the sum of fifty thousand dollars wrote on it. I was thinking I knew Toni didn't get that much money from a client. And how much did I lose out on? I just didn't even want to know.

Toni had made a killing with the business. I was mad, some of that money was supposed to be mine.

This morning was a beautiful Friday morning when I noticed Toni had gotten a beautiful black classy Cadillac. It was the prettiest automobile I had ever seen. I guess she needed some bling, bling to go with the automobile because she had a new diamond ring and, a beautiful tennis bracelet and a diamond necklace. She also bought a new wardrobe. I began to think, Toni had sold four babies when I was in the hospital. She was paid fifty thousand dollars for one baby, how much did she get for the other three? I started to think Toni had been doing this business a while now. What were her assets to this day? I needed to get focused on my assets. I had to just be cool and getting back in with Toni. I never would have thought Toni would treat me like an outsider. I was beginning to not want to be around her. She had become a stranger to me. I knew it wasn't going to be much longer before I had to move on.

Toni had three girls at the house that were between seven and eight months pregnant. I told Toni that I thought the girls came over too soon. I said it is noticeable for these teenage girls to be at the house like that. Toni wasn't hearing that. She had become so careless, I wonder sometimes if she had the hookup like her parents did. I couldn't risk this much longer. After these babies were sold I would be on my way.

It was time for me to get to work. I was feeling uneasy about everything. Toni said she had some papers with the names and the amount was to be paid for the babies. She said she buried it in the ground. I needed to ask her about that. I hoped my name is not on any of them. The only papers I saw with names on them were shredded to pieces to stop anyone from seeing them.

Chapter 36

I hear Toni calling my name. One of the girls was in labor. Toni was going to take her to the hospital soon. Her labor pains were too far apart for her to go to the hospital now. They would just send her back home until they got closer. That would give me time to talk to her about the paper trail. I went to her office she was sitting down reading something. I asked her could I speak to her for a few minutes. She said yes. I said to her I was feeling uneasy about the paper work on the business she said was buried in the back yard. She said she decided to shred all paper work as soon as we were done with it. I said ok then I went back in the living room.

I had to take Rita to the hospital. The labor pain was about fifteen minutes apart. Rita's labor pains were getting closer very quickly now. It was time for me to take her to the hospital. I needed another break from Toni anyway. She was working on my nerves very bad. I went in the hospital with Rita. I wouldn't normally go in but this time something was telling me to go. I would usually drop them off and pick them up in a few days. The nurse took Rita and me up stairs to the fifth floor to the maternity ward where they delivered the babies. Rita seemed to be terrified. She was asking me not to leave her. Rita was in a lot of pain. I could relate to that because I had experienced that pain once and I never

ever experienced it again. I envied anyone that could have children because I couldn't have any.

A strange thought just entered my head. Why don't I get one of those babies for myself? I needed to feel whole again. Not being able to have any children had made my life feel very empty.

When most men found out you couldn't have any children they look at you in a different way. As if you were less than a woman even if they didn't want any children they make you feel so low that you can touch the ground without bending down. But if you already had children even if it is not theirs they seem to have more respect for you.

Selling babies is more to me now than just making money. It's making a family. I know it's wrong but think of all the babies that were being aborted that we are saving and helping in the process of selling them a family to love. These were girls that didn't want to have babies for some reason. These were girls that couldn't tell anyone about them being pregnant but us. If we were not there what would become of those babies? I will tell you what would've happen. They would have abortions or just find a way to kill the babies themselves risking their life.

I was trying to make myself feel better or did I really believe what I am saying? I was not a kid anymore, but of course I didn't believe that.

I wanted to be able to have my own babies, even if I had to buy one. No one would know I didn't birth the baby but Toni and me. I was just being foolish. I needed to snap back into the real world.

Rita was in the delivery room having her baby. Rita did not want me to go. I was in a daze when the doctor told me that I could stay and watch the baby being born. That was an experience that would stick with me for as long as I lived.

To see a baby being born was quite an experience. I saw the baby when the head came out. Rita only had to push three times when a beautiful little baby boy was born. That was a beautiful baby, he had a pink complexion. I just couldn't hold back the tears of thinking about the time I had my one and only child.

This business is beginning to be a toll on my mental health. I just could not stop crying when I looked at Rita's baby boy. Rita wanted to know what was wrong. I couldn't tell her about what I was going through. But I knew that I needed to talk to someone. The past has come back to haunt me for I don't know how many times. I know that is a lifelong process for me because how could a person forget what I had gone through. I had to get out of that hospital. I told Rita to call when she was to be released, so one of us could pick her up.

I went home and talked to Toni about my problem. I wonder was I just being sentimental or if it was possible for me to become a mother through other means like the business we were in? Toni looked at me like I was having a mental breakdown. I thought I had that a long time ago. Then she asked was I serious? I just said maybe I'm not. It was just a thought don't pay any attention to me, I told her.

Toni made me feel like I was crazy. Actually I thought I was too, I would just let it go. I just had a temporary breakdown. It's gone now.

I asked Toni who was buying Rita's baby? She said a lady she met a while back. Toni didn't know much about this woman. That made me very nervous, but everything made me nervous.

Rita had called for someone to come and pick her up from the hospital. She just had the baby yesterday. You can always tell a person that didn't have good insurance.

Toni sent me to pick up Rita. When I went into the hospital and saw Rita's baby I began to get emotional again. I said to myself why am I going through this now? I know I have my moments but this was different. All the way home I could barely see from the tears that were forming in my eyes. Rita asked me what was wrong. I said nothing, but there was a lot wrong. We made it home safe and sound.

Toni was waiting on us with the people that were going to buy Rita's baby. They were Mr. and Mrs. Reed that bought a baby girl a while back. I was hoping no one was going to buy him. I fell in love with that beautiful baby. I was not happy at all about the baby being sold. Was I going crazy, or what? I called Toni into her office. I asked her was there any possible way that I could buy Rita's baby? She said he was already sold to the people in the living room. Then she said she was sorry but I thought you were just going through something at that time. You asked me about getting a baby of your own. Then Toni told me that she couldn't go and snatch the baby from them. She said they might cause trouble. She said she would like to talk to me when everyone was gone.

The clients left with my baby boy. I was heartbroken when they left I told Toni that I would talk to her later. I needed some time alone. I didn't want to talk to anyone. Not even Toni especially not Toni, so I went to my bedroom to lie down and I just cried and cried for a few hours.

I could not believe myself. I felt that I really did want that baby. I had never felt like that before. We had been selling babies for a while now. This was the first time I was really serious about getting a baby for myself.

It was not about the money. I just wanted a family to love. I was all alone in this world with no family ties.

I had to calm down before I talked to Toni. My mind was going a thousand miles a minute. After about two hours of crying my eyes out I went into Toni's office to see what she had to talk to me about. She told me to sit down.

Toni then asked me what's been going on with me lately. I told her I didn't know. I said for some reason my life feels so empty without a family. I just needed to love and for someone to love me back. Toni said do I think a baby would satisfy the desire to have a family? I said to Toni I really didn't know. I then said I would be ok.

Toni then said she wanted to ask me another question and that she wanted me to think long and hard about it before I answered it.

I said ok, now what's the question? Toni said so you really want one of these next two babies that were available? I was over taken by that question. But I did think long and hard for a few days.

The next few days had been hard. My brain was hurting from so much thinking that I was having headaches. I just couldn't relax. I had to think very hard.

I knew the death of Michael was weighing heavy on my mind, because I was not in the clear yet about what my future might bring. It would not be fair for me to get a baby involved in the mess of a life I had. I didn't know if I would be around to raise the baby because of this Michael thing. I was still the prime suspect.

I had to think about the baby's mother being a killer, even if it's me. I just can't live with the thought of the police arresting me and someone else getting my baby.

When the morning came I told Toni that I thought long and hard about this baby thing. I told Toni it would not be fair for me to have a baby because of this murder thing hanging over my head. I didn't know what my future would bring. So I was going to say no. Much as I wanted a baby it would be unfair for me to put a child in an unstable home. I told Toni that it was time for me to get back to business and make some money.

Chapter 37

It was time for Tam to have her baby. She had been having labor pains for a few hours now. Sara was also having pains. Sara's due date was a month away so I had to take her to the hospital so they could check to see if she was going in early. From the description of her pain it sounded like she was in labor.

When we sell those two babies I would be on my way. It's beginning to weigh heavy on my heart. I couldn't keep being in that environment with those babies if I wanted to keep my sanity. It got too hard for me. The baby selling was not going to last. The risk was greater now. With the police coming around so much we were taking a fool's chance.

I wasn't going to tell Toni that I was going to quit the business just yet. I didn't think she would like that much. I took Sara to the hospital because her baby seemed to be coming too soon.

I went in the hospital to see what they were going to do. The pain she was having was light. They didn't want them to come to the hospital if the labor pains were not close enough yet. The only reason I took Sara early because her due date was a month away. I waited to see if they were going to keep Sara in the hospital. After being there for three hours Toni called to tell me that Tam labor pains were getting very close. I asked Toni would she bring

Tam to the hospital because I was still at the hospital with Sara. While I was on the phone with Toni the nurse came out to tell me that they were going to keep her. The labor pains are close together now.

I told Toni that they were going to keep Sara. They said they thought the baby was at a good weight to be born early. When I told Toni this, guess what she said, now you can come and take Tam to the hospital. I asked Toni why she couldn't bring her. She said that I was already out. I was getting very mad. I told Toni that when I got to the house I was going to tell her a thing or two. Then I hung up the phone.

When I got to the house I looked at Toni and told her, "you are a lazy heifer." I'm tired of you putting everything on my shoulders. You have been treating me so bad lately for months now. I was just about done with you and your attitude. So you might as well take Tam to the hospital because I am not going any place the rest of the night.

Toni said that she was not going to take her either. I said well I guess she just had to call someone else. Toni said to me she was sorry I was right; she also said she would go and take Tam to the hospital. I myself being such a nice person I said don't worry I will take Tam to the hospital. Toni said she would take her. I said I would take her. I guess we are going to fight about who was taking Tam to the hospital. Of course I took Tam.

As I was getting in the car I noticed policemen were parked on our street. When I was driving down the street two more policemen flew past me. I looked out my rear view mirror and saw that they were pulling up in Toni's yard.

I was not about to go back. I was still very nervous and scared. I was still the prime suspect in the killing of Michael and Shirley. I thought to myself that that many policemen going to the house they were planning to arrest someone.

I was almost too afraid to take Tam to the hospital. When I got to the hospital I stopped at the entrance and waited impatiently for

Tam to get out of my car so I could pull off. It seemed like she was taking her time. I know that she was hurting, I was sorry, but I had the thought that the police might be looking for me.

I was on pins and needles. I didn't know what to do. I drove around town paranoid like everyone was looking at me so they could call the police.

I really needed another car to drive so I could park away from Toni's house to see what was going on. I didn't get another car but I went close to the house to see whatever I could see from where I was parked. I was trying not to get noticed. When I got close to the house I noticed that the doors were boarded up. I would guess they kicked in the doors. I wonder where Toni was. I was thinking if the police were there to get me then where was Toni. Then I started to get scared thinking that if they arrested Toni it had to be because of the baby selling because she didn't have anything to do with killing Michael and his woman.

I didn't know what to do. All my things were at the house. I just kept asking myself what I was going to do. I needed to get to a phone quick. I wanted to call the county jail to see if Toni was in it. I went to a phone booth a mile from the house to call the police station. I didn't want to be too close to the house. I looked in the phone book to find the non emergency number to the jail.

When I called the station an officer answered the phone, she said this was the local police department, may I help you? I asked was a lady there by the name Toni Williams. The officer asked could I hold on for a minute. I said yes.

When she came back to the phone she said yes they had a Toni Williams. I asked the officer what was her charges? The officer said they didn't have that information yet. The officer asked me what my name was. I had to think of a false name quick. I told her my name was Teresa Lewis. Then I hung up the phone.

I quickly left the phone booth because there was so much technology now that they knew how to trace you if you use some type of electronic.

I didn't know what to do. I went and parked at the lake to think. I didn't know what charge they had on Toni. All my things were at the house. I didn't even have a pair of underwear. I may have to forget about it if Toni was in a lot of trouble. If she didn't get out soon I would have to buy new everything. Well enough of that until I found out what Toni was in jail for.

There was no way to communicate with Toni. I couldn't get in the house and wait to see if she was going to call. I needed to get some place to think with no interruptions.

After about five hours I decided to go to Angel's house. Angel's home was so peaceful and relaxing. I had not been to Angel's house in a long time. The things I had done Angel knew nothing about them. I didn't want Angel to think I was a monster.

When I got there Angel was so happy to see me. I was even happier to see her. When I went into the house I felt a since of calmness.

Angel had her life all together. She had a husband and two children. I wonder with a husband and children around why was there so much warmth and peace.

If I had this life to live all over again I would do things differently. My life was a bloody mess. I talked to Angel for a few hours. Angel was as loving and friendly as she could be.

I guess I was the one who chose the life I lived. I know I can't go back. I am always thanking Angel for being such a good friend. Most of all I thank God for giving her to me for a friend.

Angel cooked my favorite foods. I was eating like it was going to be my last meal. That's what I was thinking. I knew the police would be looking for me too. About the business Toni and I had. Either way I was screwed.

I needed to find out Toni's charges. So I waited for two days, I then called the police station to see what her charges were. When I called to see what Toni charges were a lady answered the phone. She said this is the Police Department how may I direct your call? I said to the lady I was checking to see if you have a Toni Williams there?

I knew she was there because the last time I called she was there. I then said what were her charges? I almost hit the floor when she said she had outstanding parking tickets. You could have sold me for a half of penny with change coming back. Then the lady said she would be released in a few hours. I was so glad that I was going to be able to get my things. I waited to the next day to go home.

It was morning time I woke up to the smell of bacon, sausage, eggs and biscuits. When I was at the table Angel asked me what I was going to do today. I said to her I need to take care of some business. I told Angel I needed to be on my own. Angel said you are welcome here anytime. Then I hugged Angel and said I love you and I will talk to you later. I was on my way to Toni's house. I had been very careful to ease my way to my house when I was on Toni's street. I didn't see anything going on. I even noticed that the doors had been fixed. I had to knock on the door because Toni had gotten new locks also. When Toni came to the door she said come on in. So I just went in. Toni said where are the girls? I said the last time I saw them they were at the hospital. Toni then said did you pick up Sara from the hospital? I told her no. Toni said why not. I said Toni I was on my way to pick her up but I saw the police going to the house and I was afraid that the police were waiting on me at the hospital. Toni was so mad. I asked her what she wanted me to do. Toni said what was she going to do? She said she had two clients waiting on a baby. I had told them I would have the babies in two days. Toni also said she knew that I was a screw up. I said to Toni I got things that I also need to do. I am angry myself I told Toni. I am not going to be walking on egg shells. I think it's time for me to get going. I decided to tell Toni I was going to get myself a house of my own. Toni asked me why I was moving. I had to tell her how she had been treating me. I told her I was not comfortable being there because of her attitude. Toni asked me to forgive her. She started to cry. I was not prepared for her to cry.

I told Toni I was sorry but it's time for me to move on. Toni said would you stay long enough for us to sell two more babies? I asked how long would that be without anyone being pregnant? Toni said that she had two girls that were pregnant and one adult that cheated on her husband and was eager to get rid of her baby. Toni said she was seven and a half months pregnant. I said it would take that long? Yes Toni said.

I didn't want to stay that long. But, I said OK Toni I will stay for two more and that's it.

I often think about what if my life time crush was not so into all these women that had to be skinny and look like a beauty queen and gave me a first look that I may not have been in all this mess. He would have saved him and me a lifetime of aggravation if he would have chose me instead of all those nut heads. I still love him to this day.

My friend Angel asked me about her being addicted to a man for so many years that she use to go with and can't stop loving him after twenty five years. I responded, what about being addicted to a man you never touched or even gotten a hug from that never did give you the time of day, Now Angel I said, top that one. Angel said forgive me, yea you won, I can't touch that one.

Chapter 38

It was Saturday night Toni and I decided to go out to a club. We both got our hair and nails done. We got new clothes. Toni suggested that we go to this club called Nubian Queen. Toni never asked me to go to a club with her before, but it was nice of her to ask me.

I wore a red low cut dress with short sleeves. I had to always wear clothes with some kind of sleeves because I was not a size seven like Toni was. I wore black pumps and a black clutch purse. I took my time putting my make up on. I wanted to look good and I did.

Toni wore a knee cut pink dress suit. She wore black pumps and a black purse also. Toni had her makeup flawless. We looked so beautiful.

We had a nice time. Toni danced almost the four hours we were there. I danced a few times myself.

Toni and I had men buying us drinks the whole night long. Toni fell in love on the dance floor and I fell in love at the bar with the bar. I normally would not drink but the way my life has been going I better be living it up before I get caught.

They had a big collection of alcohol and snack food. We had a good time. I didn't want the night to end.

I was becoming intoxicated. All of a sudden all the men begin to look good. Even the man that I danced with that I thought looked like a monkeys butt. His name was Donald Glover. He tried to talk to me all night long. I finally gave in. Why not? I wasn't trying to get married.

Donald was not attractive, but his personality was charming. That's the kind of man women need to be aware of. That false charm will get you in deep trouble if you are not careful.

My new friend was telling me about his life. He would hold a conversation that would keep a girl interested.

Donald was not a tall man. He was about five feet ten inches. I had a weakness for a tall man. Donald was not as tall as I liked a man to be, but he was OK.

He said he was thirty seven years old. He said he had never been married before. He also said he had an eleven year old boy that he didn't get to see much because his mother moved to another state. I asked Donald did he want any more children, he said no, unless he got married. That answer gave me a chill through my whole body.

He asked me did I have any children. I said no. Then he flipped the record around on me. He asked me did I want any children. I didn't want any more problems. I told him that I was unable to have children. I didn't notice any surprises in his facial expression. I didn't know how to take that. We got off the subject about children.

Toni was still on the dance floor. She seemed to like the man she was dancing with. I tried to get her attention, but she was enjoying Herself quite a bit, so I left her alone.

Donald asked me for my phone number. I had been through so much I didn't need a man in my life. I gave him the number any way and he gave me his.

Toni was so hyped. She didn't want to go home. After drinking so much I didn't care where I went.

The club was about to close but Toni didn't want to go home. Toni's friend wanted to take us out to breakfast.

Donald and I and Toni and her friend went to IHop. I ordered some pancakes, sausage and scrambled eggs with cheese. I liked IHop their breakfast was very good. I liked the different flavors of syrup they had.

It was now three a.m. I was beginning to get tired. I wanted to go home. Toni and I said goodbye to the gentlemen then we headed home.

Sunday morning came around quickly. Neither one of us went to church. We were very tired from the night before. Around one o'clock in the afternoon, Toni and I decided to cook a nice dinner. Toni was having her friend from the club over. She asked me did I want to invite Donald. I said no. She asked me why not? I told her I didn't know that man. Besides I didn't want any company today. Toni kept saying to me to invite Donald. To stop Toni from getting on my nerves I told her OK.

I got the phone and called Donald. When I dialed his number the phone began to ring. It rang four times before he answered it. I said hi and told him who I was. Then I asked him would he like to come over for dinner. I said I knew it was short notice and maybe he had other plans. Donald quickly said that he would be happy to come over for dinner. So I told him to be at Toni's house at six p.m.

We had cooked meatloaf, candied yams, fried cabbage, hot water cornbread and fried okra. For dessert, I made a caramel cake and a lemon meringue pie.

Toni and I wanted to look nice when the men came over for dinner. I put on a pants suit. Toni wore a pretty dress. We put on makeup we looked nice.

I was nervous because I was a little drunk when I met Donald. I was nervous to see him when I was not drunk. It was a quarter to six. The boys were to be here in a few minutes I told Toni I had to go and check to see if my make up was OK.

We had the table set. We had put on some jazz. The volume was low so the atmosphere was relaxed.

I heard the door bell ring. I became very nervous. I went to the door and it was Donald. He did have enough intelligence to be on time. He even brought a bottle of champagne.

When I looked at his face I wanted to get drunk all over again. He was a sight and it was not a pretty one. When I got pass the shock I said hello and come in. I asked him how he was doing. He said OK and he asked me the same. I couldn't say what I was thinking so I said fine. As I was closing the door Toni's friend was pulling in the driveway. I said Toni your friend is outside. She came from upstairs to open the door for him.

Toni's friend was handsome. My friend was plain and unattractive. The only thing that looked good was the bottom of the champagne he brought with him.

Donald had a body that you might get over his face. The main thing was he was so polite and dashing and a gentleman. His conversation was interesting. All I had to do was get past his face.

We sat at the table to eat. Donald did pull out the chair for me. Donald said everything at the table looked good. I fixed his plate. Toni fixed her friends plate. Everyone seemed to enjoy everything. After the main meal it was time for dessert. Donald said he had never had caramel cake before. Toni's friend had never had it before either.

Donald said my Lemon Meringue Pie was better than any he had ever had. Everyone was to full to eat anything else. When we were done eating we went to the living room to watch a movie. I was having a nice evening. I was enjoying Donald's company. Toni and her friend went to her room. I was not about to go to my room with any man. I was not ready to make that move. I didn't know if I liked him like that yet.

I was getting very tired. I was ready to go to bed. I was hoping he would say he had to go before I had to tell him to leave.

After about nine PM Donald said he had to get going. He said he had to get to bed because he had to go to work. He said he liked to go to bed early so he could be well rested.

I got up and walked him to the door. He was a gentleman and asked me could he kiss me goodnight? I said that it would be OK. Donald kissed me on my forehead. I didn't know how to take that one. I then said goodnight then he left.

Toni and her friend were still in her room. I went to bed so I didn't know what time Toni's friend went home. When I got up I noticed Toni's friend car was still in the driveway. He had to have spent the night with Toni. When Toni got up she cooked a big breakfast for everyone. I was almost happy Jack spent the night because Toni had never cooked that good before. There was so much food. It was like a holiday breakfast. She cooked ham, sausages, bacon, biscuits, eggs, grits, hash browns and we had assorted flavors of syrup like IHOP serve. To drink we had coffee, milk and orange juice. Toni really out did herself. Jack was very impressed. I was so amazed; Toni all of a sudden became a master chef. I knew why.

Sometimes a girl gets all kinds of talents to catch a man. Then after we got him most of the talents seemed to take a long break. After a while most men turned out to be no good anyway. I must say us women need to re-think some of the things we do also. We were not all the time the right one. Men just could be so cruel and devious and just didn't care about how they hurt a woman's heart and have us women scared most of their life to trust a man.

After Jack left I helped Toni clean the kitchen so Toni could tell me what happened last night. Toni was being so secretive she didn't tell me anything about Jack but he was nice and they didn't do anything but watched TV and went to sleep.

Chapter 39

It was time to get back to work. Toni had a few girls lined up. But I didn't know who they were. Toni mostly made the first calls to the girls. There was a girl name Cee Cee that Toni called. She was eight almost nine months pregnant. Toni said Cee Cee was coming over to the house so she could talk to her. Cee Cee was to come over to the house at four PM. It was only about one in the afternoon. We still had a few hours before she got there.

Toni had this married lady that wanted to get rid of her baby because her husband was over the waters fighting for his country and she got pregnant. He has been overseas and the timing was all wrong for it to be his baby. This lady's name was Tasha. She didn't tell Toni her real name. That was OK we would rather not know their names anyway.

Tasha came over at one thirty. Tasha was a pretty lady. She seemed to be a little on the inquisitive side for me. I didn't like that at all. I called Toni to the side and told her that I had a funny feeling in the bottom of my stomach. Toni said she's OK, and I was just being paranoid. So I told Toni Ok. We went back in the living room. I was still getting more and more queasiness in the pit of my stomach. It would not go away for anything but Toni was not hearing it.

Mrs. Tasha wanted to sell her baby instead of giving it to us. Toni and I were not in the business of buying babies, we sold them. Toni and Tasha did come to a mutual understanding for Tasha to get fifteen hundred dollars for her baby.

I didn't want to be in that transaction. I was not feeling this woman at all. Maybe I was just being too paranoid like Toni said. Whatever it was I didn't like it.

It was approaching four o'clock quickly. It was time for Cee Cee to come.

Toni said she had a few buyers she had to call. Toni said she had a woman that wanted a baby boy as soon as possible, her name was Mrs. Johnson. We may have to do some switching around of the babies to make sure Mrs. Johnson gets her little boy. Mrs. Johnson is kind of an intimidating woman. I wish we were not dealing with her. She put a lot of pressure on a person. I will be happy when she gets her baby boy. There is also this woman name Mrs. Ross. Mrs. Ross wants her husband to have a junior. She is final about that. Where was Toni getting these people that were putting all this pressure on us?

It was a very nice day outside. The sun was so beautiful. The birds were holding a tune as if they had rehearsed a song. The leaves on the trees were so pretty. The grass was like a deep green. The squirrels were climbing the trees looking for an acorn to eat. This day was the first day I had saw a black and gray squirrel. They were very pretty. This day was going alone smoothly. Today was particularly nice. I couldn't quite put my finger on it but something felt like it was going to happen. I would just have to see what was going to happen if anything.

Toni had gotten up all excited about the day. I was ready for almost anything to happen.

Tasha had called Toni to let her know she had her baby. Tasha said she went into labor to quickly to call. Tasha had a boy. There were two women that wanted a boy. The both of them were so demanding. I was not sure which one we needed to get out of our hair first.

Toni decided to sell Mrs. Johnson this baby so she could be on her way.

I was beginning to have this uncomfortable feeling in the pit of my stomach. These few days had been going alone so smoothly. It was just too strange for some reason. There was that red flag going up in the air again. I told Toni again that something was wrong. Again I was just being paranoid, like I was a few days ago and nothing happened. I said ok but that I didn't want to work with Tasha at all. She got upset with me but I didn't care.

Tasha's baby weighed nine and a half pounds "wow." She was going to be released today. When I got up it was another nice day. But it felt much like the last two days, like something was going to happen. Didn't anything happen like the last two days. I guess I was just paranoid like Toni said.

Toni and I got ourselves together for the day, the phone rang. It was Tasha she said. Tasha said she had been released from the hospital. It has been two days since Tasha had her baby. She must have had good insurance. These days they release a baby out the hospital when they were barely 24 hours old. Tasha said she has a ride to the house. I was very suspicious about someone else coming over to the house, but Toni was ok with it. I would be so happy when this whole transaction was over so I could release some of that anxiety. Tasha was pulling up in a taxi cab. I didn't know why she had a taxi to bring her to the house.

It was two weeks from the day that my insurance money from Michael's death was to be released. I had knots in my stomach the closer it got to that day.

When Tasha got there, Toni gave her fifteen hundred dollars for the baby. Then Tasha left. Toni said see, didn't anything happen. I said yeah you were right. Toni called Mrs. Johnson so she could get her baby. When Mrs. Johnson got there she gave Toni thirty thousand dollars. Then Mrs. Johnson went on her way. Toni gave me five thousand dollars as usual.

The stress was all over with Tasha and Mrs. Johnson. I was very happy about that. I just had to wait for Toni to sell one more baby so I could be on my way. It would take a little while. Cee Cee never did come over. We never knew what happened to her.

Chapter 40

Today was the start of the seven day count down from the year I had to wait to collect my insurance money. Waiting for these few days to past by was a lot more stressful than the whole year was. I couldn't believe I was going to get all that money.

Every time I heard the phone ring I got uncomfortable thinking it was bad news. When I saw a police car I would get so nervous that I could barely drive when they were behind me. I was really being paranoid. I guess that's what goes with doing wrong. I was going crazy trying to get past these few days.

My life was so messed up that, it was time for me to do something different with my life, again. When I get my own money, I just might start over in another state. That will probably ease my mind about the police watching me. I needed to find a new business to get into without Toni. I was ready to be on my own without anyone else.

Every time I thought of all this money I had a smile on my face from ear to ear.

I went to the store to buy some things that I needed for when I moved. I set up an account in my friend Angel's name just in case something was to happen.

It was down to six days of getting my money. The day was beautiful. The birds were singing. The sun was beautiful and bright. The news said that there was rain in the forecast later that afternoon. I guess I wouldn't be washing my car. Looking at the sky you couldn't tell that it will rain today. There wasn't a cloud in the sky.

I went to the matinee movies so I could have a little time to do something alone. I watched a movie called "Till Death do us part." That was a movie I could relate to. I was trying to do something to get my mind off the money I was going to get.

I wished I even put more life insurance on Michael. When I think about what Michael had done to me, I wish I would had let him live a little longer just to torture him more.

It's five days away now. The day was cloudy with moister on the trees. The birds are quiet. It supposed to rain throughout the day. Toni had been singing around the house like she had just won the lottery. I couldn't say the same. I was on pins and needles. I had to do something to keep my mind occupied.

Toni got a call from a girl name Naomi. She was seventeen and nine months pregnant. Toni said she would be coming over in a few minutes. This would be the last transaction I would be making with Toni.

I had a few things to do today. I had to go on the other end of town to look at a house to buy. Buying a house to call my own had me on a natural high.

When I got to the home that I was buying, the present owner was already there. He was a nice older gentleman. His wife had passed on. That's the reason he was selling all of his assets. He was asking fifty five thousand dollars for the house. He wanted me to at least pay one third of that in advance with the remaining balance in five years. He would like for me to make a decision about buying the house within a month.

There were four bedrooms with two bathrooms, a large living room, a den and hard wood floors. The front porch was what got my attention. It was closed in with windows all around it and a big yard in the back. The outside had light blue aluminum siding.

I wanted to think on it for awhile. It was time for me to be going back to the house. I was very nervous when I saw policeman near the house. When I got close to the house I noticed a few strange cars were parked on the side of the streets. When I got to the house Naomi was there. She didn't look like a teenager to me. But she did look like she was about to burst.

Naomi and Toni were discussing what they were going to do when she had her baby. I was in the kitchen looking for something to eat when all of a sudden I heard a knock on the back door. When I looked out I saw a lot of policemen. Toni went to grab a lot of papers to put them in the shredder. The only thing I could do was open the door. When I did, five of the policemen rushed through the door asking for me and Toni to arrest us for having an illegal baby selling ring. They didn't say a word about Michael's and Shirley's death.

The policemen had cuffed Toni and me then they went through the whole house looking for paperwork. Toni said she didn't keep much paperwork in the house. One of the policemen got some papers from out of Toni's trash can. I didn't have a clue what was on them. When the officer put me in the patrol car I began to panic when I saw Naomi talking to the policewoman.

When we were in the car I saw the police locking up the house. They drove us to the police department. When we made it to the police station guess who was the top cop on the case? The lady I kept telling Toni I was not feeling her. Yes it was Tasha. Her real name was Janice Hudson. I kept telling Toni I didn't want anything to do with her.

Officer Janice Hudson was not pregnant. The baby she had belonged to one of the officer's friend. They had it set up that Mrs. Ross would get the baby. It was a perfect setup.

Toni was taken to a different room than I was in. We were being questioned by different officers. I was glad they were not arresting me for Michael's death. The case of selling babies was enough.

The next day after we were arrested we went to court to be arraigned. The judge gave Toni a ten thousand dollars bond. I was puzzled by not getting a bond for the same crime as Toni. They even postponed my court appearance.

My mind was running fifty miles per hour. I just didn't understand. I knew I had to find a lawyer quick. Something just wasn't right. Toni was already at home.

I asked the officer what was going on. They were ignoring me. Everyone was being quiet about something. It was four days before the deadline for the insurance company to release my money and I was locked up in a small room with a bench nailed to the wall and a steel toilet.

I called Toni's house collect. She wouldn't accept the charges. I began to panic. Something was very wrong. I tried to call Donald to see if he would go to Toni's house to see what was going on. I needed to know why she wouldn't take my calls.

Donald said he would go over to Toni's for me. I asked him would he try to get an appointment to visit me. He said he would do what he could. He said he wanted me to tell him what was going on. I didn't want to discuss any of this mess; I seemed to always get into.

I knew I needed to tell him something. I needed to convince Donald that I only had a small part in all this mess. I need him to take care of a few things for me. I needed someone on the outside to be my eyes and ears. I really needed to know what was going on with Toni.

I was going stir crazy. I wanted to call Angel but, I will not be able to face her with what I had done. Angel had been there for me whenever I needed her. I was more worried about Angel knowing what I had done than the authorities. Angel might say she was friends with the devil. I just would not know what to say to her.

I have been in jail for two days now. No Donald, No Toni. No anybody. I have been calling but Toni will not accept the charges. I don't know anyone else to call.

I have to go to court today to be arraigned on the baby selling charges. I wanted someone to be by my side when I see the judge.

I still could not get Toni on the phone. After thinking long and hard I decided to call Angel. I had to call her collect. I know she will accept the charges. I hope when she accept the charges and I tell her about the baby selling business that she will still be my best friend.

I asked could I use the phone. They said that I can only make one phone call. I didn't know what to do, I was so nervous about calling Angel that I kept dialing the wrong number. I had to ask the guard to dial it for me. When I finally got Angel on the other end I heard the operator ask do you accept the charges from Lagretto Watts. Angel said yes. She said hello to me, then she asked me where was I? After shaking so badly I finally got out that I was in jail. Then the big exploding question came out. Why are you in jail? I thought my heart was going to hit the floor. After I took a deep breath I said to Angel, do you remember me telling you that when I was a kid that my parents bought me when I was born and that my friend Toni's parents was the people that sold me to my parents? Angel said yes. I then said that Toni and I had the same kind of business. Angel said are you kidding. I said I wish I was. I said to Angel, Toni was in jail also but she's out on bail now. I don't understand how she could get out so quickly and it's been two days and I had not seen the judge as of yet. I told Angel that I was going to court today and could she come and be there when I see the judge? She said yes. I had to see the judge at four o'clock. I didn't understand why they had me to see the judge so late in the day.

I was on pins and needles waiting to see the judge. I was yet trying to get Toni on the phone. I couldn't even get Donald on the phone anymore. I didn't know what was going on.

As I was waiting for four o'clock to get here I read the bible they had in the holding cell. It's true that when most people are in trouble they start to read the bible a lot. I was trying to do anything to pass the time along; when about three thirty an officer came to my cell and told me my court day had been cancelled for today. My heart started beating fast. I asked why had it been changed and changed again and until when? The officer said he didn't know why or when.

I had to hurry and call Angel before she left for court to let her know that my court date was cancelled.

Angel asked did I want her to make an appointment to visit me. I told her no, I just needed some time to think. I told Angel that I would call her as soon as I heard when my next court date would be. When I got off the phone with Angel I begin to panic. All kinds of things were going on in my head. Toni got out of jail the same day. They seemed not to want to give me a bond for the same crime. I didn't understand this at all. I felt it was time for me to be contacting a lawyer. I didn't have anyone that would have my back and contact a lawyer. I had to rely on strangers that were in the holding cell with me.

I contacted a lawyer named Jonathon Jackson Jr. The women in the cell with me said that Mr. Jackson Jr. was a real good lawyer but he was expensive. I could have gotten a court appointed attorney, but people say they were not good at all. I knew from experience they were telling the truth about that. They said with a case like I had I needed to have my own attorney that was ruthless and with a good winning record.

I made an appointment for the next day. I needed Mr. Jackson Jr. to find out why they haven't given me a bail yet. Mr. Jackson said his first visit was free but after that session it would cost five hundred dollars a day. I almost used the bathroom on myself. I didn't know what to do. I had some money but I didn't know if I needed a high priced lawyer yet. I didn't have much of a choice if I wanted to find out what was going on with my charges. I desperately needed some answers to the questions I had in my head.

I had Mr. Jackson Jr. come to see me so I can get some answers to my charges. When Mr. Jackson Jr. came to see me he said I had a charge of baby selling and what he heard was that they were working on another charge against me. When Mr. Jackson Jr. said that I knew I had to retain him as my lawyer so that he can get the ball rolling.

As I was talking to my lawyer he asked me was there any other charges they may be able to bring against me. After thinking a few minutes Michael popped in my mind. My heart almost felt like it stopped. There was no way I was going to tell my attorney I killed my husband. If they are talking about charges for the murder of Michael I might as well drop dead.

Mr. Jackson Jr. said that he would have to dig a little deeper to find out what else was going on. I really needed to talk to Toni now to see if she had heard anything about other charges they are talking about. When I called Toni I was baffled even more to find out she had changed her phone number. Then I called Donald's number. Oddly enough Donald's number had been changed too. I thought what the hell is going on. I didn't know what was happening. I didn't know what to think. Who could I turn to? Angel popped in my head. I wanted to call her so badly but I was so ashamed to face her. If I could close my eyes and wish for my heart to stop I would have.

All I could do was just sit and wait for my Attorney to find out what he can. I needed some ears on the outside to find out what was going on. The only thing I had to do was to pay that high priced lawyer to do all the work for me. It's hard when you don't have many friends to help you along the way.

Tomorrow is the deadline for the insurance company to release my money from the policy Michael had took out on him.

The next day I called the insurance company to see when they were going to release my money. They said something to make me feel like I was in another world. They said when they checked with the police department I was in the county jail waiting to be charged with first degree capitol murders of Michael Watts and Shirley Thompson. I couldn't believe my ears. Then they said if a charge is pending they can delay the funds until the outcome of the case. I thought what else could happen to me. I wondered did they get any information from Toni on me killing Michael. Toni had been a close friend but lately she wasn't acting like it. I hope she didn't tell them anything. It also turned out that Michael had all his assets going to

200

his parents. I was mad as hell. He is where he needs to be. Lord help me, as if I was worthy of his forgiveness.

It was now the fourth day I've been locked up. It was now time for me to see the judge. When I got in the courtroom the only person came to support me was Angel. There was no Toni or Donald. My lawyer was there, when they called my name I stood up with my attorney. The prosecuting attorney stood up and said the charges against Lagretto Watts were illegal baby selling ring and First Degree Capitol Murder of Michael Watts and Shirley Thompson. When they read the charges I collapsed to the floor. When they helped me up I looked at the facial expression on Angel's face. It was a look of disbelief. I just hung my head low. When Angel walked out of the courtroom before the proceedings was over I knew I had lost my best friend the moment I needed her the most. I didn't blame her for not wanting to be friends with a killer.

I was all alone. Everyone I knew had turned their backs on me. I had only the hired attorney Mr. Jonathan Jackson Jr. It seemed like I was just doomed. All the things I had done seemed to be coming back on me tenfold. What was I to do? The only thing I could do was to sit and wait.

The judge gave me a million dollar bond (cash). I was unable to post that large sum of money. I just had to sit and wait to see what was going to happen. I had no clue to what evidence they had on me for killing Michael. The only person knew about what I did was Toni, but she wouldn't tell anyone about me killing Michael. Toni and I had been friends for years. We had some disagreements but none that would make her turn on me.

As I was sitting in jail, not having a visitor since I had been locked up, I read a lot, mostly the bible. I knew I was a monster. I was not fit to live any longer. I was a criminal. I couldn't even produce any off springs to carry my name on. I sometimes wished I knew where the child was I gave away many years ago.

It was three o'clock in the morning when I woke up from a bad dream. I dreamed Toni was going to tell the police about the evidence I had hid in her back yard. I even dreamed that Toni had taken everything I had. I knew all the same it was just a dream but I was yet terrified just the same.

I had been locked up for three weeks. I was ready for them to do whatever they were going to do to me. My lawyer said they had a good case on me for the selling of the babies but he didn't know what evidence they had on the murder charge.

My trial date was quickly approaching. They said they were going to hold the First Degree Murder Charges First. After the murder charges they would try me for baby selling. I been paying my lawyer all this money and it seemed as though nothing was being done to defend me.

When I saw him he said they had some solid evidence on me for the murder of Michael and Shirley. I asked him what evidence. He said he didn't know just yet. He said we would find out in court the next day. I didn't know I had a court appearance the next day. My lawyer said they had to present the evidence to see if there was sufficient enough evidence to try me for murder.

When the guard came to my cell to get me I was nervous. I didn't know what to expect. When I walked in the courtroom to my surprise Toni and Donald was there. I was so happy to see both of them. I sat at the table with my lawyer. The prosecuting attorney's name was James Calvin Jr. He was known as the punisher because he almost always got his man. He had put more people behind bars than any other prosecutor before him. They said Mr. Calvin Jr. had some very bold tactics to get his man. That made me nervous.

The judge asked the prosecutor to call his first witness to the stand. I almost died when he called the name Toni Glover. I thought they just got the name mixed up. It dawned on me that Toni had married Donald. I became enraged with hate. I was ready to commit another murder.

Donald just looked at me with this mean expression. I was beyond hurt to know that Toni and Donald stabbed me in my back and twisted the knife. I had to get a grip on myself. I didn't need the judge to see how violent I could be, so I composed myself.

The bailiff asked Toni do you promise to tell the truth and nothing but the truth so help you God? Toni said yes. Then she sat down. The prosecutor asked Toni did she know Michael Watts. She said yes. Then he asked her to tell the court what kind of person he was.

Toni said he was a very nice man. She said he always treated her nice. He was well liked by everyone he met. Then he asked her did she know me. Toni said yes. Then he said tell us a little about Mrs. Watts. Toni said that she and I grew up together in Arkansas. Toni then said I used to be her best friend. I didn't understand why she would say that so dry. Then Toni said I was a nice person at times until someone crossed me. I was hurt by her making that statement. Then he asked Toni what was her relationship to Michael Watts? Toni said they had a brief affair after Lagretto and Michael had split up. I was breathing fire. I should have killed her. I couldn't believe my ears. What a friend. That has happened to me a few times before. I had this one girl that lived near me that I called my niece; she was cheating with this man I had been with and cared for. I met him down south and he came to see me and I had taken a few trips to see him. After I was gone for a while he was coming to see her. These back biting dogs are treacherous. You'd expect that out of a man more that a woman back in the day. But now these women are worse than these men, you'd expect them to have some self respect. Yes, I am talking about you Henry and your female dog. I have been forced not to trust anyone but my best friend Angel. Yes you other women that I hung out with I don't trust, but I love you, but trust, "NO"

Anyway! Then he asked Toni did she know anything about the killing of Michael Watts and Shirley Thompson? She said yes. Then he said tell us what you know. Toni talked about how I talked about killing Michael. Then she said I told her where I had hid the knife that I killed Michael with. I was floored by what Toni was saying.

She had diarrhea at the mouth. She was singing like a bird. Toni was so hostile against me. I didn't understand why at the time.

Then she went on to say that she had put away the bloody clothes that I was wearing the night I killed Michael. I was shocked to find out she had put my clothes away that I was wearing the night of the killing. Toni had gotten me good.

The prosecutor said to Toni why are you so upset with your friend Lagretto Watts? Toni said that she has been upset with me since the day she found out I had her parents locked up years ago. I could have turned a flip at that moment. I didn't have a clue Toni was holding a grudge all those years. I couldn't say anything I was in shock. All I could think of was if by some miracle I was to get off. I was going to kill Toni and Donald for planning to hurt me.

The judge said there was enough evidence to proceed with a trial. If Toni hadn't said anything they wouldn't have had a case. Man I wish I could kill her.

When Toni left the stand smiling I asked could I say something to my "friend" Toni. They said yes. When I got in front of Toni I asked her why she did that to me. She said she had been waiting years to find a way to pay me back for turning her parents in. She also said she made a deal with the prosecutor that if I gave them you my charges would be dropped to a minimum of twelve months in jail. Then Toni said you know my husband don't you? She was so lucky my hands were cuffed behind my back. I wanted and needed for both Toni and Donald to die. They had set me up good. Now I didn't have a leg to stand on.

After leaving the courtroom I was so enraged with hate for Toni and Donald, but there was nothing I could do behind bars. I was now ready to fight to get out of jail so that I could have my revenge.

After a few days of calming myself down I was now ready to get to work on my case. My lawyer and I had to think of a way to get Toni so that she won't be able to testify or a way to make her out to be incompetent. My trial was to start in four weeks. We had to work hard and fast.

My lawyer was now doing his job. He was gathering up names and evidence that would make Michael out to be an abuser. Jonathan my lawyer want to work on Toni most of all. He asked me how Toni got my blood stained clothes. I said I didn't know. Then he asked about the buried knife. I said I don't know. I didn't want my lawyer knowing I killed my husband. If I told him the truth he might not defend me with everything in him. I didn't want him to have any doubts about defending me the best he knew how.

Jonathan and I spent a lot of time together. He would come to see me mostly every day.

It was now time for my trial. I have been sitting in jail for three months. I was ready for anything. I was not surprised to see Toni and Donald in the courtroom. I had already prepared myself for them being there. The both of them had smiles on their faces. I guess they wanted me to see how happy they were. I was trying not to let them make me lose my temper, so I tried not to look at them.

As the trial got underway I didn't realize how much evidence they really had on me. Thanks to Toni they made me out to be some kind of monster. All I could do was to just wait and see. I had to question myself about what type of person I was. I didn't think I was as bad as everyone made me out to be. I just believe that some of these Michael's and Shirley's should be put out of commission so women with self-respect can live in peace and harmony. I must say I was a little out there back in my day when I just wanted to hit it and go. But I made it a rule never with one of my friends or ex-friends men.

The first person they called to the stand was a police officer. The bailiff asked the officer to raise his right hand. Then he asked him, do you plan to tell the truth and nothing but the truth, the officer said yes.

The prosecutor asked the officer was he dispatched to an address at 252 Dyson Dr. The officer said yes. The prosecutor asked what did he see when he reached the home of Michael Watts? The officer said the front part of the house was engulfed in flames. The prosecutor asked how long it was before any other emergency service arrived. The officer said about three minutes.

The officer volunteered the information that he watched as the firemen got the blaze under control. The prosecutor asked the officer how long it took the firemen to put out the flame. The officer said about fifteen minutes. Then the prosecutor asked did he go inside and if he did what did he see? The officer said it took a few hours before anyone could go inside the house because it was still too hot for anyone except the fire department to go in. Then the officer asked did one of the firemen say anything to him about the fire? The prosecutor said that one of the firemen came out to tell him that it was a homicide because there were two bodies tied up and were dead in a bedroom.

After the house was safe enough to enter, the officer said he and his fellow officers went into the house. He said as he approached the first bedroom at the top of the stairs he saw a woman in a chair tied up and gagged and soaked with blood. Then the officer said there was another victim in bed tied up and gagged with strange cuts all over his body.

The prosecutor asked what was so strange about the cut marks. The officer said it looks like they were a lot of small cuts and that it appears that there was salt and pepper all over Michael Watt's body. The officer said that it looks like Mr. Watts was tortured before he died.

Listening to all the testimonies made me sound like I was a crazy nut. If I was, I was driven to it by so much abuse.

After all the officers were done talking bad about me it was time for Toni to take the stand. I must say I was so nervous about Toni taking the stand that I almost passed out. I wished I could kill her on the spot. If I knew for sure they were going to find me guilty of murder. I would have.

When Toni said she swear to tell the truth I wanted to spit on her but then it appeared that there was so much of the truth she had on me that she didn't have to tell a lie. I suddenly got sick to my stomach.

Toni was telling everything she knew about me killing Michael and Shirley. She definitely had diarrhea at the mouth, dirty tramp. That's a "friend" for you. Toni told them exactly where I had buried the knife at. She even told them about me telling her that I had just killed Michael and his woman. I sure did set up myself, good.

I was so hurt to see my real friend Angel listening to all the bad things I had done that I wished I could just disappear. The looks she had on her face will stay with me forever.

As the trial was nearly over I realized that not one thing good was said about me. I might as well give up; I didn't have a leg to stand on. It took three days for all the testimony. All we had to do was wait on the jury's verdict. Waiting on someone to determine your life was a hard thing to do. I know that when you do wrong you will pay. If not immediately it will come, believe that.

I was sitting in my cell reading my bible when an officer came to take me to the court room because the verdict was in. I could have had a heart attack. I said a quick little prayer and the officer handcuffed me and took me to the court room so I could hear if my life was over. I stood up with my lawyer the judge asked did the jury reached a verdict. The foreman of the jury said yes. The judge asked what the verdict was. The foreman said in the verdict of Lagretto Watts we found the defended guilty of two counts of first degree murder of Michael Watts and Shirley Thompson. The judge asked each one of the jury was this their verdict? Of course they said yes. All I could do was look at Angel and say to her that I was sorry.

The judge set the sentencing for two weeks later. The officer led me back to my cell. All I could think about was Angel. I could see that she was so hurt. It was now another waiting period for me now. The only thing I could get was life without parole. There was no death penalty in Michigan. I didn't know why there has to be a waiting period for the sentencing when there was only one thing they can give me.

Well the waiting was all over. It was time for them to officially sentence me. The judge asked me to stand. Then he said this was a heartless crime and that the way the victim was killed he wished there was a death penalty, but he sentence me to life in prison without any possibility of parole. As I was listening to the judge I was thinking about how my friend Toni set me up or how I set myself up with her help. I wanted to see what was going to be her punishment for selling babies. I was now at my permanent, temporary relaxing place for now. I had a lot of things to think about. I was trying not to think about Toni and whatever his name is, that I couldn't focus on my own salvation. I started to read a lot. Of course, I became a Christian while I was on lock down. I guess if I really knew what that meant. Maybe I wouldn't be sitting here now.

I will not relax until I find out what is going to happen to Toni. I had a lot of time to think. With all I was trying to do I could not get Toni out of my mind no matter how hard I tried. Toni was stopping me from thinking clearly. I wanted something to happen to her. Every time I think about Toni the Lord jump in my space in my head. Much as I have done it seems like I would put all that behind me and focus on getting to heaven on a technicality or by his forgiving grace. But the devil was constantly riding my back.

It had been a few months since I moved into my new home. I was doing my daily exercise, when one of my roomies came to me with a newspaper and told me to read this. I became so upset when the paper said that Toni had been sentenced to six months in the county jail. Before I knew it I was throwing things around that I had to be locked down in the hold. I was as mad as hell. It felt like I was breathing smoke through my nose. I just couldn't believe that she only got six months. I was now going crazy. I had to compose myself so I could get out of this hole. That Toni, she will not even get a number because she didn't have to do time in a prison.

After I was put back in regular population I started to think more about what I could do to get even. I decided to call my lawyer to check on an appeal. I didn't know if I had a chance or not but I wanted to try anyway.

The Devil was drilling Toni through my brain. It was like I was losing my mind. I had begun to read about forgiveness. I wonder if a person can be forgiving with as much as I had done. I just don't know where to go from here. I wanted revenge and then again I wanted my soul to be saved if, it wasn't too late. I know that I didn't want to burn forever. You that suffer from depression, mental, physical and sexual abuse, broken relationships and all other problems that you let build up in your mind you better take this advice from a front row seater.

What's going to happen with my life the next go around? Please get some help before you snap and it's too late. I don't want anything like what happened to me by my own doing because I didn't get any help I just held in all that hate and it destroyed me. I am just starting to be sorry for what I have done. Don't you be sorry when it gets to be too late for your freedom. Seek Jesus; no matter what you have done God is alive. I just didn't put him at the head of my life and look at where I am seeking him, in prison when I could have seeked him being free. I am now a big time girl in a big time prison. Stupid isn't it? "Well Yea".